TAPED SEX HISTORIES

TAPED SEX HISTORIES

Case Studies in Variant Sexual Practices

by

CARSON DAVIS

The Borgo Press
An Imprint of Wildside Press

MMVII

CONTENTS

INTRODUCTION

As a writer of fiction novels, many dealing with sexual themes, I've found both men and women will openly talk about their sexual problems with me. Perhaps this is simply because they believe that a writer, in general—and one who deals with the sexual side of life—is shockproof. The fact remains that without any personal desire to enter into such intimate conversations with almost total strangers, I have over the years managed—through the normal course of my profession—to gather actual taped conversations with people who have sexual drives which, to them, seemed depraved or different. One might call such people, driven deviates.

In the following pages the reader will be exposed to the stark, detailed confessions of some of these people I have known—though, in order to protect them, their names have been changed and in some cases the circumstances surrounding their lives, These frank and sometimes startlingly detailed sexual experiences might tend to shock those readers who have not been exposed to such open boldness about a subject that is considered by many as the most romantic and Spiritual state of being, and by others as a degrading and guilt-ridden part of their own lives, which they do not wish to even admit to themselves.

The people in this book are in many ways much the same as most people around the world; they are also exceptions in that they have been able to talk about their experiences, guilts and frustrations—the first step to full understanding of oneself. In most cases I suggested they seek professional help—some did and found the proper adjustment in life, others managed to find their own answer, some failed; a few I have lost contact with and have no knowledge of what became of them. All were people desperately seeking someone to talk to, to listen quietly and not be shocked or revolted by their stories; all realized to some extent, consciously or otherwise, that one of Nature's best healers is just the simple act of communication with another person, finding understanding that maybe they were not much different than anybody else,

Possibly the people reading this book will find a little of themselves in one or more of those who passed through my life, for a moment, and spoke of themselves. Maybe the reader will also learn that sex, like all other bodily hungers, must be fed; but to feed the sexual hunger in a healthy, mature way is to understand oneself and the needs of the partner who enters into such an intimacy.

If I learned anything from these people it was that the word deviate is a much misused word and that there is no truly deviate sexual person, only people with shades **of** different colors, mixed in different ways with each person. The only deviate is the person who does not understand their drives and thereby feel's guilts which are founded only by ignorance of themselves and others; and this person becomes a driven deviate who is torn by his or her desires and ignorant fears, which are in reality night shadows in darkness, haunting the mind like ghosts with no more substance than what the mind gives them,

I hope the reader will find understanding of others by the experiences of these people who now follow.

—CARSON DAVIS
1967 and 2007

CHAPTER ONE

The Man Tease: Maria

Maria is a young woman in her twenties, remarkably developed and voluptuous with wide, full hips, firm thighs, and a large sensual mouth. Long black hair flows freely over her shoulders and as she speaks she tosses her head in such a manner that the hair ripples and waves back and forth. I met her at a party and when she learned I was a writer, she began a quite brazen conversation, which had to be carried on later at my office, where we spent the rest of the night talking and sipping whiskey.

Sitting on the large leather sofa, legs crossed, Maria looked up at me and then, after taking a quick wallow of her whiskey, asked, "Where should I begin?"

"From the beginning. Ignore the tape recorder."

She smiled widely, revealing even white teeth, uncrossed and re-crossed her legs in such a manner that the short skirt slipped upwards. She pulled out a cigarette and then waited while I lighted it. The flickering flame of the match seemed to give her large dark eyes an intimate seductive look.

"You know," she said quite casually, "I was raped in my teens."

"Want to talk about it?"

She shrugged. "I guess that's the best place to start, since you said to begin at the beginning. It was some guy I had known casually in school. One of the older boys. I've forgotten his name...but I guess that doesn't make any difference." She paused long enough to take a drag of her cigarette and then a sip of whiskey. "I've never talked about that. Not to anybody. Funny how I'm able to talk to you about it." She shrugged again, tossed her head and then smiled. "I guess I'd been asking for it for a long time. I developed quickly here," and she touched her large breasts, "and the boys got big kicks looking at me. I wore tight sweaters at school and got into trouble about that, one time. But that's not important.

"The thing is, out of school, I'd wear tight sweaters, which cut low, to give a good view of the swell between. It was fun noticing the looks boys gave me. I hardly knew what they were after or what they wanted to do...not then. I was too young and innocent. I know now that they wanted to suck them."

She was wearing a very low-cut, tight-fitting dress that night and I could easily understand any man's desire to fondle and kiss those large breasts.

"I would thrust out my breasts, hands on hips, shoulders back, just daring the boys. And, imagine, without even knowing what I was daring! How innocent children can be!" She laughed throatily. "Then one night, coming home from a late movie—just about a half mile from home—I crossed to-

12

wards the park, which was a short cut to home. I'd hardly entered the park when suddenly this boy loomed up from the shadows. God knows where he came from. What the hell was he doing there, I don't know! But he looked at me, grinned. Said something like, 'You sure have big cans.' I guess he was drunk. Probably was, come to think of it. He reached out for me, said, 'How about a kiss?' Just like that. Then suddenly he was kissing me. I struggled, but he was very strong. I started to scream and he slapped me one hard. 'You be quiet or I'll really slug you!'

I was scared green. He fairly ripped off my sweater, while yanking me into the darkness of some shrubs. There he pushed me down on the ground, yanked the sweater high above my breasts, then went wild in his frantic attempts to get my bra off. Then he started sucking my breasts, real hard. I begged him all the time to leave me alone. He slugged me once or twice, I don't know exactly when. It's all sorta blurred. I remember him sucking until I ached. Then he fumbled with his pants, pulled my skirt up, fairly tore my panties aside and suddenly he was into me. I wanted to scream, but was afraid. He kept at it for some time and then seemed to get his orgasm. Like I said, I don't remember much about it. He was hitting me with his body, that big thing shooting in and out like a knife, then suddenly I was alone."

"What did you do then?"

"I cried. Then I went home. The boy was picked up by the police. I don't know what happened to him. My mother was terribly upset—my father wanted to kill the boy. I was just numb."

"Did you get any pleasure out of it?"

"Nothing. Just pain. Numbness. Just the emotion of terror. I didn't know what was happening. Hell, I was just a kid."

"What kind of effects did it have over you? I mean—did you change about your reactions toward boys?"

"A little. It was a long time before I would date a boy. I wouldn't let any date touch me—but they sure the hell wanted to." She laughed, stubbed out her cigarette and then said: "But finally the numbness wore off and I discovered that it was fun to tease boys. I enjoyed it more than ever. The biggest thrill in high school was to let them touch my breasts. I'd even take off my sweater, some times, let them work off the bra, and then tell them if they touched me I'd scream. I would have screamed, too! And I guess they knew it."

"When did you experience your next sexual relation with a man?"

"When I was much older, in college. There was this guy who worshipped me. He followed me around like a little dog. Then one day he asked me out on a date. He wasn't very good looking, but for some reason I accepted. After going to a movie, he took me back to the dorm. On impulse I suggested we go to Make-Out Point—that was a place above the little college town. We drove up there and I was getting a real kick the way he kept giving me sidelong glances. I didn't plan on letting him have me. I just wanted to tease him a little—no, correct that, I think I honestly wanted to tease him a lot. The closer we came to our destination the more determined I was to go as far as I could in teasing him.

14

He was fairly shaking by the time we found a parking place.

"I said, 'You want to kiss me?' and he was quick to say yes. 'What'll you give me?' I asked. He really looked surprised. I don't even know what I meant by that, so he could hardly know. I said he could kiss me. His tongue was large in my mouth the minute our lips touched. He pressed my breast with his hand, caressingly. On impulse I did something I'd never done before. My right hand slipped between his legs and explored. It was the first time I had ever really touched a man like that. He was getting hard, fast. And as my fingers felt its shape it grew harder and harder.

"We broke the kiss and he gasped something about my being so great. I asked 'Do you want me to touch it again?' He merely nodded. I guess he was so shocked at my offer that his vocal chords were knotted up. 'Why should I?' He reached out and placed his hand on my crotch, totally covering it. I immediately slapped it away, said, 'I asked you a question. Why should I touch you like this?' and my hand caressed his shaft. 'Tell me and I'll touch you again,' He gasped out something, which didn't make much sense but pleased me quite a lot. I touched him once more, this time squeezing the tip between my fingers.

He moaned, his eyes half closed. I withdrew my hand and waited, pleased by his reaction, sorta feeling good all over. It was fun teasing him that way. He opened his eyes, said: 'Come on, baby, don't stop now.' I laughed at him. 'I'm not in the mood.' He seemed to blanch, then cried: 'You're kidding?' I shrugged, and then said: 'I bet you would like me to take it out. Wouldn't you? I bet you'd like me to take it out and keep caressing it. Wouldn't you?' With each word I spoke, I found my own excitement building, especially because he was really shaken. 'Is this what you want me to do?' I asked, reaching out and touching his zipper. 'Want me to pull it down? Want me to really give you a thrill?' He lunged at me. 'Are you kidding, baby? Stop putting me on. Either get on with it or forget it. I'm dying. Please, honey, don't leave me like this. Come on, stop saying all those things. Do something.' The pleading in his voice struck a hot cord inside me, deep and I wanted to touch him and tease him some more. Hell, I was man hungry, but didn't know it. I pulled down his zipper and after a little struggle, during which he helped like hell, I was holding him in my grasp. He looked at me with wide eyes, then down at my hand. 'Baby, your hand feels great. But do something with it. I don't...can't stand this.' I laughed and then thumbed the tip of his shaft and he moaned, trembled. 'Baby, let's get naked and do it!' I gave a flat no to that, squeezed hard on that large shaft and then released my hold. I was now really getting excited. It was the first time I'd ever experienced such orgasmic excitement. Teasing him that way was what turned me on! Yet I was kinda frightened and all that. I mean, having a dick like that in me...and that first time...well, that wasn't a nice sensation. Not at all."

She looked probingly at me, saying: "Do you have any idea what a man's big...well, hard feels like...I mean sure you do. I'm sure you've touched yourself plenty enough. Like all the men. But I mean, do you have any idea how it makes a girl feel

16

inside, all shivery and hot. Damn moist. If you want to know the truth. Just the idea of one doing me can make me so hot that I could rape the man." She giggled as if delighted at the way she'd said that, as if wondering what effect it might have on me. Then she simply leaned back, pleased with herself and said: "Well, I really wanted to go all the way, of course, but was afraid. I sat back, away from him. He just stared at me as if I'd hit his face. Then he reached out, grabbed me, kissed my face, lips, worked his hand under my sweater then under the bra. After a moment I pushed him forcefully away, said: 'Okay, if you want, I'll get naked to the waist, You can *look* at my breasts. But just look!' He cried: 'I'll do one hell of a lot more than that,' I merely shook my head and then pulled the sweater off, reached around my back and unclasped the bra. He gaped when he saw my naked breasts. 'You want to kiss them, don't you? I bet you'd do anything I asked, just to touch them. Make my nipples really hard!' But, of course, you bet they were hard. Real tight, hurting knots. "Like what you see?" I asked, without any offering in my voice. He said: 'I want to kiss you all over, baby,' I laughed again and then reached out and touched his cock once more…."

She broke off there, studied me in a rather amused way and quickly said: "I hope that doesn't shock you."

"What?"

"Saying cock. Calling a man's dick a cock! You know."

"Not at all. What ever turns you on."

"Oh, I don't know about that. You wouldn't

want me to get all turned on, now would you?" She winked playfully, giggled, squirmed and sighed. "Well, I grabbed his big one, you know, his cock...oh, lovely hard, hot cock...and he had one lovely in my hands, and I squeezed hard, hoping I'd hurt him. He grabbed at me very suddenly, like, like I couldn't even stop him. Even if I'd really, honest and truly wanted to. But I...the feel of his fat dick was so charmingly thrilling I wanted to play with it all day. I could do that, you know. Just handle, fondle a man's prick for hours. Toying with it. Just sliding and slipping my fingers all over...well, I guess you get the message and all that. Of course. Well, this young stud wasn't all that sophisticated, like you might be, I mean. He was all over me, like a beast gone wild. I must say. Thinking back it was some trip. No woman I swooned out of control. Oh, his lips were sucking one of my breasts until its nipple grew hard as the meaty shaft in my hands. I was all the time holding that big stick like I couldn't get enough of exploring its just marvelous shape. I mean, like it gives me the shivers just remembering. I moved my hand up and down so fast, and he was just about groaning in his joy of what I was doing. I had no idea how that can drive a man beyond control. You know what I mean. *Ooops!* All done! Even then, though, I knew enough to stop when he leaned back. I was so hot. I can tell you. Hot to simply devour him. I couldn't stand it any more, but I didn't let on. I leaned over him, looked at the large swollen hardness between his legs and before I knew it I was doing it. You know, kissing. I wanted to know how the end felt against my lips. Oh, what a divine sensation. Like hot rubbery velvet, so soft and padded and...."

She broke off, shivering, eyes racing all over me as if wanting to act out her words on anything within reach. "I can tell you...man alive. What a send-off that first time was! And you better believe he was in joy heaven, moaning and groaning and begging me not to continue. Saying things like 'Oh, baby, take it in...oh, yes, do it again...oh, you're... so good!' And that just kept me at...well, I was getting as much as I was giving. He was out of his mind by now, I guess. It felt good in my mouth. All at once I was so excited I couldn't stand it any more. I leaped away from him, and struggled out of my panties, pulling my skirt up around my waist. A girl can get so hot and wet there, in her...in her pussy. Pussy wet all over. It was really burning. Deep inside I as burning all over. I couldn't wait to feel him in me. He wanted to grab me, but I pushed him back. He shifted and then, legs hanging over the side of the seat, he let me have my way. I straddled him and then felt his shaft against my love-hole, oh so soft and hard and hot, yet velvety. 'Baby let's do it, come on, I can't take it much longer,' he pleaded and I grabbed his shoulders, lifted upwards and then slowly I started to lower. If he hadn't directed himself right on my warm, moist you know what, I would have missed completely! The wild pleasure of that long shaft slowly entering me was so great that I screamed out, clutching tighter upon his shoulders. It went in deep, so deep I thought it would come up through my mouth and almost wished it could be at both places at once." She laughed at that point, then made a side comment, "I've done it that way since then. It's fun that way...I mean, two men. One down there, just churning my butter barrel and the other gripped right here!" She placed three fingers into her mouth and slowly moved them in and out to illustrate her point, as if that were necessary. All the time her eyes were greedily probing mine as if hoping I'd reveal some uncontrolled desire to be doing to her what she was describing.

Slowly, almost lingeringly, she withdrew her fingers, dropped her hand between her thigh for just a moment, winking at me in a very playfully seductive manner.

"I'll tell you." Her voice said huskily, "If you want, I'll do you before the evening's out. I like going down on a man. I mean I *really* like it!"

She lighted another cigarette and then continued: "Finally, of course, he couldn't take much more and then exploded. By that time I was going off myself and afterwards I made him drive me home, as if I were mad at what had happened. Boy was that jerk jerked out of his skull, worrying. He kept pleading that I understand and that he really hadn't been able to stop himself. He just kept saying 'babe, I'm sorry...couldn't help it. You're sooooo hot!' Later I really laughed my head off about that. If he'd been experienced at all, and not such a dope, jerk, he'd have known I'd had more orgasms than he did. Men just blow their wad, women just keep swimming and swimming. In fact when he was pleading for forgiveness I was cumming hearing him say all that to me."

"Did you see him again?"

"Never! I wouldn't let him touch me again or date me. That was very important. One trick per

20

dick, I suppose!"

"Did you feel guilty the next day—hate him?" She shook her head. "Hell no, I wanted to find me another stud to tease. It's always been like that. A guy has to beg, has to really be begging to get me turned on. Like if *you* wanted me, you could have me do anything to you—just so you begged, so that you really were so excited you didn't give a damned what you said." Maria at that point pulled up her skirt. She touched her crotch. "Wouldn't you like to touch my pussy, kiss me wet there, feel the hot moist warmth of me around yours?"

I smiled and said that we were there to talk about her.

"Why don't you get naked and I'll go down on you, but you'll have to beg...you know that."

"I'm not the type," I told her quite forcefully. Though the idea of having sex with her was intriguing. But I would not beg a woman in the manner she suggested.

"I guess we don't turn each other on," she announced quite casually, though almost sadly. "It's a shame."

She shrugged again and continued telling me of her further sexual experiences, each time going into as much detail as before, obviously with the aim of getting me so excited that I would beg her to get naked. Each experience repeated the same pattern as the first man she had seduced. Each time she needed to punish a man into pleading for her—then she would get turned on. One experience revealed the ideal situation to her. She had been picked up by a couple of men and she stripped down naked before them in a hotel room. She told them to strip. Then she started caressing each man's penis with her hands and once she had excited them just to the point where they wanted her, she took one, directly, and watched the other watching what was going on.

"This turned me on fast. I liked watching the other stud. Boy he wanted me but bad. Afterwards I was so excited that I even let the other do me. But this is the only time I ever allow men to have me without pleading."

Maria is one of those people who did not want to change. She saw nothing wrong with her sexual habits. In fact it was the thrill of her life to get men so wild to have her that in no way would she considered any change of style. She actually laughed at me when I suggested that she seek professional help.

"Are you kidding? I like it this way. I have a lot of fun and kicks. So...some guys don't turn on that way—that's just fine, but there are others that do and there are enough to keep me happy."

COMMENTS

I've lost contact with Maria. In fact I only heard about her once, after the conversation, from a friend of mine who testified that she was everything she claimed to be. Apparently he had been turned on by her manner of love making.

Maria is what might be called a man hater, but highly sexed. In order to excuse her erotic desires, she forces the man to plead, she punishes him for the first man who raped her—and then she enjoys what follows. The sad thing is that she did not want help. She will never find a normally happy marriage. The man she will marry will be a slave to her demands—her opposite. But the idea of love and tenderness will be impossible until she learns to understand herself, forgive what happened to her as a child and forget the past, living the present with a man who could love her for herself. But she will hate men for as long as she continues to refuse professional help.

There are many women like Maria, who are not quite as bad, who find happiness in marriage, but who could, if fully understanding themselves, find even greater happiness. The sad thing is that many do not realize they are this way, that they have a little of "Maria" in them, and therefore never seek professional help—and thus miss out on having the total happiness with a man, which could be theirs merely for the seeking.

CHAPTER TWO

The Call Girl Man: Frank

Frank has been in the motion picture industry all his life, working his way up from shop boy to film cutter, casting director, director and finally producer. He's not one of the big boys, and the line of business has nothing to do with him other than the fact that it, like others, gives men a chance to have their pick of some of the most beautiful women in the world, whom he flatly refuses to touch. He's a heavy boned, square jawed man who talks in a gruff sounding voice. His hands are large, his manner that of a man who seems to know exactly what he wants, yet there was something about him which, during the interview, struck me as subtly nervous, not the kind of nervousness which comes from a high strung type of person, but rather a sort of wiggling—a mental and emotional struggling that revealed itself in short little chopping actions of his right hand. He seldom smoked while we talked.

I had met him through a friend and over a couple of drinks one evening we began talking about sex, and when he learned that I was putting together a book on the sexual experiences of people I called driven deviates, he offered to give me some real "stuff" if I wanted it,

We made an appointment in his plush Hollywood office, where I set up my tape-recorder. He offered me a drink, which I took only because I have found that most people will talk more freely once they have relaxed with a cocktail. Unhappily, I discovered that my host needed nothing to drink and did not have anything.

Sitting in his swivel chair, leaning back, pressing his large hands together, Frank said: "Well, what kind of stuff do you want?"

"It's your party, Frank," I told him, setting the mike closer to him. "This doesn't bother you, does it?"

"The mike? No, I'm so used to them in my profession that I don't even realize they are there," he pointed out, making me feel like an ass. "I guess you want all the dirty stuff."

"Whatever you want to tell me. As I said the other day, I'm putting together a book on the sexual experiences of people who fall in a different kind of category. I'm not interested in mere sex stories, the kind told in men's locker rooms. I'm not interested in the normally balanced relationships between a happily married man and wife. They have it made, as we all know."

He nodded like a wise profit, then made a jerky motion with his right hand. "Well, then, to get down to the very meat of it"—he laughed as if at a private joke—"I got laid when I was young enough not to really even know what a cunt was for. Don't say I was illegal. Wouldn't want to give the wrong impression there. Even if it used to be pretty common for young guys to make it with some experienced woman…the dream fantasy we all had at one time or another—and heard about, but never really knew much about. Anyway. I was a dumb kid first time around and she was one naughty lady."

"That often happens."

"With me it was a much older woman," he stated, nodding at my comment. "Until then all I knew about sex was that I could go in a corner and play with myself. That was just about it. I'd heard very little about what really went on between men and women. My parents were the kind of people who wouldn't talk about sex; it was a dirty word to them. All I knew was that I could play with myself and have one hell of a ball."

"What happened with this older woman? How did it take place?"

"In her living room. She was divorced from her husband and I guess a little horny. She was about…oh, I guess thirty-five or so. Dark haired, on the plump side—no, not plump, just not very tall, and well developed. She had a small mouth, dark eyes, rounded, though not slender, shoulders and arms. She was dressed in a bathrobe that morning. I often talked to her—just casual conversation— usually on the front lawn. It wasn't until she split with her husband that she took more interest in me. At first it was just more prolonged conversations. I would imagine she was building up to what finally happened, but wanted to go about it casually—or, who knows, maybe she wasn't consciously aware of what she was leading up to. Though at the time…I mean that day it happened, she was quite direct in

26

her moves. She knew exactly where things were leading, and with that professional maturity of an adult who knows about sex and knows how to go about exciting a man, she went skillfully towards her goal."

"How did it happen...I mean, just exactly how did she manage to get you into—"

"Into the house?"

"Yes."

"One of those conversations. I had just come home and it was a pretty hot day. She called from her front door, through the screen, as I passed her house, telling me that my mother had gone shopping in town. I attended classes at the community college. She asked if I'd like to come in and have some coffee and cake with her. It was the first time she had invited me into her house and though I was surprised by the offer, several things worked on me to make an automatic acceptance to the invitation. The folks didn't let me drink coffee. I liked the idea of that...rebellion against though parent authority and all that. Even at that age...I was dominated by my folks, I guess. Still staying at home. They dictated that if I wanted to stay there I had to follow their rules. Of course I drank coffee when with my friends...but this was different, right under their 'noses' so to speak! I would imagine, she was fully aware of all that cause we'd talked a lot about that. She wasn't a deeply religious lady and somewhat intellectual. Read a lot of books. So she knew what she was doing. Very calculated. Probably planned for some time. Her every move that day was calculated."

"Had you ever thought of her as a sexual object?"

"Not until that day."

"Did you later?"

"Hell yes! I'd dream about doing it with her and then go into that 'corner' and play out my own dirty little sexual fantasy."

"What happened after she invited you into the house."

"She took me into the kitchen, where there was a breakfast nook. We sat there and drank coffee and ate some cake she had. She sat next to me, fairly close, though at the time I wasn't aware of the meaning of that closeness—it was part of her seductive move.

"I sometimes wonder, now, how dumb could I have been. Hell I knew about girls, I mean, in my mental dreams. I was still very, very shy. And somewhat backward, at the time. No dating experience, either. A big too young for my age. But I sure as hell was alive to females. I mean my hormones were ready willing and able to function! In fact those ol' hors were moanin' all the time!" He chuckled at his pun, then went on: "Well, I was dumb. Let's face it. And, until that day I hadn't thought of the Mrs. Well...call her Mrs. Jones... don't like broadcasting real names, you know. Not nice doing that. Away, I just thought of her as the lady living next door. A non-sexual sort of person. A friend for a long time. But, well, she wasn't about being non-sexual that day!"

"You believe she actually invited you in to have sexual intercourse with you?"

"I know damned well she did!" he exploded, again jerking his right hand in the air. "Hell, she went about it like a real professional—and I should know about the professional tramps! They come to my office all the time. They think if I get goodies from them they will get some part in one of my pictures. Hell, they get the surprise of their lives. I wouldn't touch them with a ten foot pole."

"Why?"

"The whoring little sluts think they can wind me around their little bodies and get what they want. They just don't get it. Oh, I'll let some of them play out their little act, even get naked in front of me. But then I pull the stop."

"Because of your wife?"

"Wife?" He sounded puzzled for a moment, then his face softened. "I have a wonderful wife both in bed and out of bed."

"Then you're happily married? You don't desire these women who come offering themselves to you, stripping naked and—"

"Hell, what do you think I am? I'm not a queer. I get excited as all hell! But I won't touch them. I call up some pro and have a session with her."

"Prostitute?"

"Yes."

"Yet you say you are happily married and that your sex life with your wife is good."

"*That's* beside the point."

"It doesn't bother you to cheat on your wife like that."

"With a prostitute? Hell, no!"

"Well, continue with this first woman."

"She started talking about college, at first, then girls. Just casual things like, 'Have you any girl friends?' I had some girls that I talked to, but I was a little frightened of them. From my answers she obviously guessed that I was girl shy. She asked: 'Don't you like girls?' But I didn't understand the question and sorta mumbled out something about not knowing what she meant. Then she said: 'Well, don't you find their bodies interesting?' I told her I was like every other guy...sure I liked their bodies. 'Then you find a girl's breasts exciting to look at, isn't that right?' she asked. Her robe somehow managed to part just slightly at the top. Maybe it was parted all the time, but with her question she touched her own breasts, drawing my eyes down to that point. I could see, from my position, the naked curve of a large breast, though not the tit. I assured her that I liked a girl's figure. What guy didn't? Then her next question really popped the cork, 'Ever seen a woman's body before?' Well, I hadn't, but I said I had. 'Pictures?' she asked. I nodded, That much was true. But they were art pictures, paintings of the old masters and I'd been made to feel guilty."

"You mean you'd never seen any girlie magazine pictures. Or even *Playboy* centerfolds?"

"Well, no. Like I said, I was a real weird guy. Even at that age. Not that I didn't grow up fast, mind you. I mean, I was a slow starter, and I caught up once I started."

Somehow his words lacked conviction. I had no way of knowing. But he talked as if he were telling a story about a young teenage boy being seduced by the lady next door, rather than a college age man. Still, there are a many people who never have sex before marriage, for a number of reasons, good and bad. In fact, everything he was telling me might

30

have been a lie.

I don't think it matters how much truth was being offered, or how much colored and altered for the moment. What counts is what a person tells me, real, imagined, or outright lies. The underbelly of their minds is what counts; and this is what offers up the words. Cover ups are common under such conditions. It is like a bunch of guy getting together and bullshitting about all their experiences while having never had any experience at all, except in their imaginations.

"Dirty magazines? Looking at those pictures? You got to be kidding." He broke off as if that didn't even sound convincing to himself. "Well, maybe I saw some…don't remember." That sounded very evasive. "You see mother said that such pictures, even in art, were not very nice. But she also stated that in art it was all right to look at them, because I should have an education in the art of the old masters. Well, anyway, this woman asked: 'Ever seen a woman's breasts?' By now I was beginning to get restless—a reaction which I now know to be the first itching of sexual excitement. She pulled aside her robe to expose one breast, 'A child suckles on a woman's breasts, you know, like the animals.'

"I guess I gaped in shocked surprise. My mouth was hanging open, because I'd never seen a woman's breasts—not even my mother's as a child, because she bottle fed me. That naked breast, large, full blown and with a huge nipple, started the blood pressure throbbing in me. I didn't know what was happening, but I knew I felt much like the way I felt when playing with myself. Her thigh touched mine and I could feel that it was naked. She had in some manner managed to pull up the robe high enough to expose her legs, though they were hidden under the table. She smiled and asked if I had ever wondered what a woman's breasts felt like. I nodded. Then she said: 'Would you like to find out?' And before I could answer she offered: 'You may touch mine— then you'll know.' She reached out and took my hand, which was trembling by now, and placed it against her breast so that the palm covered one large pink nipple that grew rigid very quickly. I would imagine, considering what I know about women now, that she was highly sexed. Or hoary as hell! Her own breathing was getting a little rapid and that breast pumped against my hand. 'What do you think about a woman's breasts?' She asked the question in a husky voice. I don't know what I said, but probably something to the effect that they were soft. 'You know, Frank,' she told me, quite casually I remember, 'a woman likes to be touched on her breasts. It feels very good. Do you like me?' I said sure. 'Do you like me *very* much?' she asked, still holding my hand against her breast, harder now. I was literally speechless, with a hurting hard so big and throbbing that I wanted to jack off right then and there. But, of course that was quite impossible. Actually, I remember, wondering how I could get out of there and go off and relieve myself…didn't even think of banging this woman right then and now! The thought didn't even enter my mind."

"Are you pulling my leg?" I chuckled. "Surely…."

"Not at all."

"Didn't even wonder?"

32

"Well, I wasn't dumb, if that's what you mean. I knew, also, a little about sex, not anything right on the button, so to speak, but a guy's imagination does what's necessary to make a...well, when he's masturbating he'll picture something sexy and female and all that. Sure. I began to think how I'd imagine her breasts when I was jerking off. That kind of things. But I had not idea...what was about to happen."

"And that was...."

"Well, what do you think? Hell, man. She was out to take me not only into her home but right into the depths of her womb! Whack. whack, like that!" He slapped his hands together to illustrate his point.

"So she was asking questions about if I liked her or not. Obviously, exposed like she was...hell, what red-blooded young man wouldn't be liking what he was seeing. I nodded, unable to really speak very well. 'I like you a lot, Frank. I would like you to do me a very big favor. Would you kiss my breast—like a child would kiss a mother's breast?'

"I was so startled by the suggestion that I just sat there, unable to move. I mean, I knew what she was asking, but didn't relate it to seduction bold and simple. It was that ol' Mrs. Robinson bit—almost right out of the movie." He chuckled at that. "I did want to kiss her breast, but I didn't know why. Then she asked me, 'Does it excite you to touch my breast? Do you like the idea of kissing them?' I nodded. At that point she dragged me onto her breast, wiggling against my lips until I felt the nipple between them getting so nice and hard. She murmured in pleasure, then moved me away, looking at me like I was a delicious dinner for a desper-

33

ately hungry woman. I didn't really know what was going on, but I felt excited as all hell. 'Come on, Frank, come with me.' She slipped out of the breakfast nook, and her robe was flowing open and I could see that velvety darkness between her legs, at the bottom of her stomach. It surprised me that she was so different from boys there. I'd never really seen a woman like that before, remember—and those pictures are not very revealing. Air brushed and all that, of course. And the arty stuff, well, that was highly selective and you didn't see no damned hairs. She took my hand and then led me into the living room, closed the front door and then stood in front of me, opened her robe, 'You see, this is a woman's body. Do you like looking at me?' I didn't need to answer and she didn't expect it. She said, 'I like to look at a *man's* body like you like to look at mine.' And she reached for me, her hand unbuttoned my shirt. I was totally paralyzed. My pants felt like they were seven sizes too small. She said, while undressing me, 'You have such a good build. You are very hard all over. I can't think of you as anything other than a man to want, to desire, to hold. Does that surprise you? You're such a dear.' That last, of course, was her way of admiring my hard on. Her words had been calculated to keep me paralyzed while she stripped my body. Once the shirt was off, she undid my pants and reached down to see just how excited I was. That's when she moaned in breathless delight: 'Oh, so lovely. And so big!' Those knowing fingers played my cock up and down. 'You like that?" she inquired with a smile. 'Want me to kiss you there? Just like you kissed my breast?' And before I could so much as move, she

34

was on her knees before me, and going down on me. And believe me she went at it as if she was wild about…well she just…did me up good! Like any guy in such a situation, I came in a matter of seconds. She loved it. And her lips didn't stop for a moment.

"When I was hard again, she moved away and smiled up, said: 'Now I'll show you something else.' And hell if she didn't take me right there. She led all the action. I remember her hands directing my cock into her already wet pussy. I was out of my mind and to be truthful I don't really remember too much of what happened after that. I was in a daze and was taken like a fire consuming a dry summer forest. Afterwards, she told me never to tell what we did."

"What happened after that?"

"I went home in shock."

"Did you ever tell your parents or friends?"

"No. Never! I was both shocked, guilty and frightened, too. It was our secret until years later. By then, well, it doesn't matter any more. And I don't reveal her name even now, today, so many years later."

"Didn't you want to do the same thing again with her?"

"Yes, but she never gave the offer and then moved away shortly afterwards."

'When was your next experience with a woman?"

"A prostitute. I was much older and in my last year at college at the time. A bunch of the guys wanted to go to a local whorehouse. So we went to a house which was fairly well-known and each took our turn with one of the girls."

"Want to talk about it?"

"Why not? I got a redhead, slightly built, but with nicely shaped breasts. She couldn't have been more than twenty-eight. She took me to a small room in which a large bed awaited us.

"'How do you want it?' she asked. I said, 'Why don't you take the lead?' She nodded, quickly slipped out of her dress, told me to be undressed. Then she got out a bowl and washed my cock. She seemed quite determined to make sure I was well cleaned, but at the same time managed to arouse me. Most prostitutes are fairly careful about this—or, rather, the ones who are smart and professional about their business. Then she went around the world with her tongue and wound up screwing me—woman on top. She didn't waste any time, but got it over with as fast as possible. Afterward she told me to get dressed."

"Did you enjoy it?"

"Not really, come to think of it. Well, comes the wrong word. Or, rather, I did come, of course. But it wasn't thrill number one. She was too cold-blooded about it. A cheap pro is out to get as many men as possible, done and over with. They really love the idea of suckin' the sucker off quite and fast, at out the door they go! I've learned that a call-girl is far better,"

"In what way?"

"Well, you can control everything. You're pay- ing bit bucks. They will give you more time if you pay more money. All night sessions can be wild. And, mind you, if you know how to handle them."

"In what way?"

"Well, a smart call-girl will get it over with fast if the mark is a sucker. They like having control. Really. The man thinks he's in control, but…. On the other hand if you play it smart, you say, fifty bucks for a quickie—but, baby, I'm giving you a twice that and a very big tip if you're really nice and good."

"I see what you mean!"

"I learned this some years later from a friend. We called up a couple of girls and had them come over to the apartment we shared. We had drinks, conversation, then this friend of mine laid it on the line. 'Look, girls, we have fifty dollars for you, if you do a good job.' They laughed at him. The one I had picked, a blonde with big tits, said: 'Fifty for quickies, you've already taken up a lot of our time.' We had already planned on seventy-five a girl for an all-night party. This was, obviously, some time ago. Prices are jacked up, now. I was married at the time and on location, away from my wife for months. I wouldn't cheat on her—but a prostitute wasn't cheating, really. It was better with a prostitute than going into a corner and playing with yourself. See what I mean?"

I nodded and asked: "What did your friend do after the laughter and turn down?"

"He said: 'Okay, girls, twenty-five more to split between you, as a tip—you don't have to tell your contact about that.' Again my girl said: 'You gotta be kidding.'

This friend of mine then sighed, and said as if it were breaking his heart: 'Okay, twenty-five each as a tip if you make it a good job, and all the booze you want to drink. Call it a day off—a half day off, anything you like.' Then the two girls looked at each other and nodded. My friend said: 'Okay, Frank, let's get the party going.' That was our cue. I took a bottle of gin, then led the girl into one of the apartment's bedrooms. We stripped down naked and then I said: 'You sex me up, first.' I was slightly drunk, lonely and not caring much about anything other than thrills. At that moment I just wanted her to do something; and quick.

"She laughed, asked: 'How do you want it?' I told her, 'First time, just you do all the work, and we'll see about the next time. Okay?' She nodded, said it was my party. She directly grabbed hold of my cock and started to blow me. I was still standing and suddenly the idea of letting her continue this way seemed rather exciting. When she asked if I wanted to lay on the bed I said no. 'Do you like it this way?' she asked. I merely nodded. Remember I'd been married for a few years, yet my wife had never done it that way, nor had a prostitute since I'd never had a prostitute since the first time in college.

"Later we tried several positions that night. For the first time in my life I entered a woman animal fashion. She placed her hands on the bed, bent over and I pushed against her—she seemed to enjoy herself quite a bit for the first time."

"Did you enjoy it that way?"

"I enjoy it any way with a prostitute."

"What about your wife?"

"I do it the normal way. My wife is shy and though we have a wonderful sex life and she'll do anything to me with her mouth once she is aroused enough, I've never done anything dirty like that to her."

"You think of it as dirty?"

"Well, let's say there are wives and there are prostitutes."

"You have had a lot of experience with prostitutes?"

"Call-girls. Yes. Any time some chick comes in here making a sexy offer, I call up a girl and have her come over here quick to relieve the pressure. It makes things easier."

"Did you ever think of calling your wife—or going home—or holding off until you get home at night?"

"Hell no!"

"Ever go down on a woman?"

"Yes. But only my wife."

"Does she like it?"

"Hell, yes! We've done the whole thing…you know 69's, and things like that."

"And she likes it?"

"She loves it."

"Then why not go to *her* instead of a prostitute?" I suggested.

"A prostitute will do anything on command. She will explore any position."

"And your wife won't?"

"I wouldn't ask her!"

"Why not?"

He made a nervous action with his right hand, and then for the first time during the interview pulled out a pack of cigarettes. It was a while before he answered my question. "I can't…well, we don't talk about sex with each other. I make a pass at the right moment and she plays along with the gag. We make love. That is it.

"Did you ever think she might like the same things you do? I mean—that she would be willing to explore more sexual positions with you?"

He considered that for a moment then said thoughtfully, "I never...well, would have, thought about that."

"Well, Frank, I'm no professional, but from what I've learned—for what it counts—I believe you'd be surprised about your wife. She might be everything you want—she might even make it possible to save all that money you're throwing away on professionals—did you ever think of that?"

"I couldn't talk to her about it and I won't even consider...wouldn't know how—anything different than what we've been doing. I have a respectable wife. She's no whore!"

I subtly suggested that a third party might help him—a professional being the best possible answer. It seemed such a shame that his childhood, parental guidance, and later experiences, had caused him to be locked-up tight about wives, sex and women, and thus unable to communicate realistically to the woman he had married. They were losing out on a lot of pleasures I felt they could be sharing just for the mere manner of talking about it. Communication between a couple can make the difference between a happy, wonderful relationship and a horridly limited and unhealthy one.

COMMENT

Frank, I learned, from the last conversation I had with him, had gone to a professional for help. His problems were far more complex than suggested here, dealing with deep-seated sexual guilts caused partly by his upbringing and by his first experience with the widow next door. The main problem with his wife was the lack of verbal communication. She was shy and, as it turned out, wanted to explore all by-ways of normal sexual relations with her husband but wouldn't lead him. He couldn't talk to her about sex and found it easy to go to a prostitute and make his demands without going into embarrassing inquiries or explanations. His money made the demands automatically followed without question. Once he talked to a professional about his problems, it was pointed out to him that women are much the same as men in their sexual needs and desires, but different in the way they express their desires. Sure, they experience sex in a somewhat different way, taking longer to reach a climax but able to ride through multiple orgasms stretched over a prolonged period, while the man is somewhat more direct and faster to exhaust himself. Those kinds of issues are different with different people and working out a compatible love-making routine is something all loving couples will work out between them if they want a rich and rewarding sex life.

The fact that his wife had always gone as far as he directed revealed that she might quite honestly be interested in going as far as he desired. After consulting professional help for some time it was possible for the two of them to openly talk about their sexual needs and desires. Happily, Frank is one of those people who sought out help and got it. If he still goes to prostitutes, I don't know. Possibly, when he is on location and away from his wife for a long time. But the important thing here is that he managed to find out that his wife could give him everything he was paying hard cash for —that he didn't need to go to a professional—and that their marriage was made that much fuller merely by total and honest communication between them. And by doing all this, Frank also gained the plus of learning more about himself and shucking off the unfounded guilts he had felt all his life about sex. The compulsive need to seek prostitutes was, at least, in the normal course of his life, cured.

CHAPTER THREE

The Bisexual: Judy

If you met Judy on the street, you would not think there was anything unusual about her. If anything, you would simply notice an attractive, trim looking blonde and think: "do blondes have more fun?" She looks more like a fashion model, but is a little more developed than some I have known. She wears clothing which elongates her figure. Her face is classic model, with a slightly up-swept nose; large green eyes that suggest she bleaches her hair—which is a fact; high cheek bones; a pouty mouth, the lower lip full and smooth; a wide forehead. Her body is always dressed in such a manner that her well-developed busts are kept secret, and her hips accented by flaring skirts, or merely by other little fashion tricks she has picked up over the years. She will stand with her shoulders slightly forward to keep her breasts looking more flat. She is posey, having a habit of striking standard positions that accent the suggestion that she is a professional model; though she actually worked at a beauty parlor which catered both to men and women. She can take on the attitude of total sweetness, submissiveness or frank, honest aggressiveness; depending on her immediate mood,

I met Judy through a friend who simply said she was a character for one of my books. This is a statement made loosely to almost all writers; in Judy's case it proved more than true. The introduction was made one afternoon at my friend's apartment, but that evening Judy came to my apartment for cocktails. My friend and his girl, of the moment, were with us at first. Before going into her own personal account it is necessary to indicate something of what happened that evening in order to give an insight to Judy as others saw her.

We had had enough drinks to make everybody slightly high and by the time it was 10:00, Judy turned to my friend and quite boldly said: "Don't the two of you have some place better to go?" The statement was aggressive, demanding, though not cutting or actually cruel.

My friend simply grinned, shrugged, grabbed his girl, and said something to the effect that he *did* have some place better to go, at that. He winked at his girl. I was horrified at first, because I'm not in the custom of chasing guests out—they come and then leave when they have exhausted the party and never that early. When making some awkward attempt to excuse the situation I got it from both ends. Friends say: "Forget it, we know Judy." Judy, on her part, got a little miffed: "Don't you *want* to be alone with me?"

It was then that I got the message. Sometimes even little-old-me can be a bit thick-headed. We had talked about my writing to some extent, because

Judy was fascinated by the subject matter of many of my books. Apparently whatever she had in mind had become so pressing that it was impossible to wait longer to get on with the action she so desired.

The minute we were alone, Judy turned to me, asked: "I bet you have learned a lot about sex."

I merely shrugged.

"I think you're rather cute," she announced, coming close, pressing her hips against mine, and caressing my cheek with one hand, the back of my head with the other. "Do you find me attractive?"

To put it simply: she was coming on quite aggressively.

Her lips were almost touching mine, and I could feel the points of her breasts—or more properly the bra—against my chest. I assured her that I found her highly attractive, as any man would.

"Then, let's make love," she stated flatly. "I never did like to play around the bush. If I like a man and a man likes me, I don't see why it is necessary to play out a dating game."

"Okay. Anything to make you happy," was my classic remark to that.

Stepping away, she said: "Well, now that that is settled, let's take a shower together, first, I like to make sure my lover is clean, and there is something funny about taking a shower with somebody else."

She started stripping and looked up at me in a way that would have made anybody feel like a damned fool. I undressed and by the time I could pay any attention to Judy, she was naked. Her breasts were large, rounded, the points pert, the nipples high. Her stomach and hips were beautifully shaped. She let me look at her for a moment, then taking my hand, asked where the shower was lo-cated.

The shower stall was not designed for two peo-ple, but Judy managed to make the fit seem natural. She immediately reached down and fondled my pe-nis with expert fingers until I was stiff as hell. Her actions were quite casual. She wouldn't let anything happen in the shower, but her fingers managed to keep me at a high point. Once outside she allowed me to dry her, then watched as I dried myself. Then we went into the bedroom. There she sat on the edge of the bed, grabbed hold of my hips, drew me close and used her mouth with expert care and then once satisfied that I was ready for her, she managed to get the idea across that she wanted me to enter her in that position. This was the norm for her: something different every time. She went about it in an excited manner, directing the moves, letting me know ex-actly what it was she wanted and in what fashion.

Since this book is not a confession of the au-thor's sexual experiences, there is no need to go into further detail. I mentioned the above to merely offer a picture of how she can be, from personal observa-tion. We saw each other several times before she fi-nally suggested that I tape her story. I had learned some details about her early life, but nothing like that night when she allowed me to tape the story of her sexual experiences. She was naked, sitting on the floor beside the tape-recorder, the mike in front of her.

"I never told you before, and I don't think it will shock you, but I've done it with women," was her opening remark.

"You like it that way?"

"I like it every way, as you discovered," she stated matter-of-factly. "The only thing I don't like is the idea of being trapped with one man or to put it another way, one kind of lover. I like sex and there is no *one* person who can satisfy my cravings. Obviously, because there is no such creature as a male-female with both sexual organs."

I had to laugh at that one, because the picture it invited was fantastic; though if her remark was totally correct is questionable—yet it was correct for her, since she meant quite honestly that a man or a woman alone would not be enough, and this was true, for her.

"What was your first sexual experience?" I inquired.

"You know that."

"For the tape recorder."

"Oh." She covered her mouth with a delicate hand as if startled. "Oh, how silly. Of course. With my stepfather."

"How did it happen?"

She fingered the glass of whiskey in her right hand, took a sip, then said: "I had to go to the john one day and stepped into the room to discover my stepfather standing in there, looking at himself in the full length wall mirror. He was totally naked, and had a hard on. I didn't know him very well—since mother had married him just a few months before. But he was a very handsome man, well developed, wavy dark hair, strong, but with a sensitive face. I was old enough to know something about sex and petting. But I was fascinated by that large swollen member."

"Had you ever seen a man's penis before?"

"Oh, not really. I'd...well, quite frankly, I'd touched a date's, felt its hardness. I'd let boys use their mouths on me. I liked that a lot. But I'd never seen a man naked with a total erection. I was startled, to say the least–I mean, first, to see Larry in there...anybody for that matter, since the house was supposed to be empty and for the second thing... him, and naked—let alone with an erection. He had been standing there, admiring himself. He saw me and his mouth dropped almost to the floor. He made no move to cover himself, though, and it was obvious from the expression in his face that though he was possibly startled and embarrassed by the sudden intrusion, he was also excited. I was good looking and developed enough—hell, I was old enough to have been had by then and get away with it. I'd considered it for some time. I knew mother had carried on several affairs with men before marrying Larry. I'd envied her—and Larry...well, he *was* a dreamboat. So we stood there looking at each other. Finally he managed to find his voice and said: 'What are you doing here?' I countered with: 'What comes naturally,' but my eyes found the full length of his penis and suddenly we were both laughing. Somehow that broke the ice. I said: 'You look great! No wonder mom fell for you!' He shrugged. I asked what he had been doing in there and he shrugged again as if it was quite obvious what he had been doing. I stepped close, within reach of him. 'I've never seen a man like this before.' I stared, suddenly bold. I guess the sight of him with that big thing was rousing me. I wanted terribly to touch it. I wanted like hell to do more than touch it.

"Under the circumstances there were only a few

things Larry could do. He could ball me out and act embarrassed or angry, he could walk out, or he would play it by ear. I learned later that he'd come home early. He's a salesman, you know—and finding mother away, on one of her long shopping sprees, he simply had some cans of beer. That makes some men get hard fast. He wanted a woman like crazy. What people will do when they are alone!" She laughed throatily and then kind of shrugged. "Well, in any case, I knew instinctively that he would do nothing unless I made it obvious what I wanted. It was a delicate situation and I didn't think I'd get what I was after unless I made it impossible for him to give it to me. I had to take the initiative.

"So," she said after taking a strong drink of whiskey. "I grabbed him." Judy laughed loud, then said: "He cried out, told me to not do that. I said: 'Why not?' And this time I gently fondled him. 'I've always wanted to know how it really felt, naked like this,' I announced, feeling very bold. 'I can't say I haven't wondered about you.' Somehow I knew that if I flattered his ego I could do anything I wanted with him...he merely stood there, probably shocked at what I was doing. Sensing this natural hesitation, I said: 'This could be just between the two of us.' Then when he still seemed to hesitate, I added: 'What happens between us doesn't have to be made public.' He still seemed to hesitate. What I mean, by the way, is that he just stood there, open mouthed, unable to speak. I then got real bold, said: 'Don't you want me? I prefer older men, you know, younger ones are such kids....' He choked, then finally said 'You little bitchy child. Of course I want to, come here.'

"Did you enjoy this first act?"

"Not very much really. I got a little frightened after it happened. First the fear of blood and then I thought about what would happen if mother found out and then a lot of other fears started pressing in on me. There was a sense of let down. When he went off I was merely numb. As Larry said afterwards, 'Judy, let me tell you something. The first time is never very good for a woman. And because I care about you very much, I want you to totally understand this–so just put your clothes down and I'll show you.' I started to protest, saying things like what if mother came back and found us that way. He merely shook his head, saying that she wouldn't be back for a couple of hours. And before I could really protest very much, he had me in his arms, one hand cupped my breast, tenderly, gently, thrillingly. He kissed me lightly on the lips and forehead and cheek, then whispered in my ear:

"'Now it's your turn to know total joy.' Before I knew what he was doing he had his tongue and lips between my legs, I guess I had several orgasms because of his oral lovemaking. When I felt him lift away and realized he was about to enter me, a sense of panic settled in and I started to protest. But he whispered softly to me, reassuring my fear. This time, when he entered, it was tender, slow, careful. Then when he started movement, it was slow, easy and I could almost measure the total length of him—which was pretty long! Only later, after I'd just about gone out of my head, did he start really going after me–and I guess we both got our goodies all at once. It was pretty great and from the way he

50

went about it I was assured that he honestly wanted to satisfy me. This was just about the only time he was so totally giving in his love making."

"You mean that it happened again?"

"Many times," she admitted, lighting a cigarette, puffing smoke nervously out between pouty lips.

"Weren't you afraid your mother would find you?"

"At first–but later I didn't much care any more. It had happened once and it was obviously impossible not to let it happen again. Mother went out on shopping sprees about once a week, and then there were her bridge parties and things like that. We automatically accepted the fact that when she was away the children would play. Nothing was said about it, but the next time she was gone, on a Bridge party, I really wasn't surprised to find Larry home totally naked, a can of beer in his hand, sitting on the living room sofa. He looked up at me, grinned. I laughed, asked: 'Want a piece of the action?' It was enough to make the arrangement total, and there was no doubt in my mind that it would continue."

"How'd you keep this from your mother— surely living there in the same house and all that, she must have noticed something strange something different."

"We couldn't keep it from her. One afternoon she came home and discovered us in bed. She had purposely returned home early and found what she expected to find out. I merely laughed in her face and demanded what the hell she was going to do about it. Mother was—still is, for that matter—a very attractive woman for her age...well, hell, she had me when she was only sixteen...an early marriage which ended with my father being killed in an auto accident; he wasn't much older than mother. Well, anyway, there was quite a scene...actually there wasn't anything she could do about it. But... Larry swore that it wouldn't happen again and she was so much in love with him and such a sucker for a good line—which Larry really knew how to put on—that she believed him. We continued the affair, but away from home. We met on street corners and went to a motel or just out into the country. Larry was a real bastard—still is, for that matter. He'd just love to put it to me—but I've had it with him."

"What stopped it?"

"Nothing, really. Just that I went off to college at the end of summer and that was it. I had had a guy and wasn't afraid of sex—and so that was the end of Larry. I met fellows in college. And I met girls. I mean—I went to bed with girls."

"Oh, yes, you mentioned that. Want to tell me about it?"

"Why not! Of course. That's what we're here for. Tell you what it's like for a woman to be with a woman!" she laughed, finishing off her drink and extending the glass. I got up and refilled both our drinks and then, after she had sipped hers, she said: "My roommate was a fairly attractive woman, dark hair, bouncy breasts, wide hips—and if she'd dug men she would have been popular. But she didn't give out to the boys—couldn't care less. She wanted girls and enjoyed every minute of it. I, for my part, enjoyed anything sexual—or rather was about to learned that I did."

She took another swallow of her drink and then after looking at me in a rather sensual way, which would have burned anybody up, she said:

"I knew very little about sex, really. Just petting, and things, then the affair with Larry. It was during the first—no second—night at the dorm that Carol—my roommate—got to going on me. Some booze had been slipped in the dorm and all of us had some and it was my first experience away from home with any liquor. I felt a bit high.

"Carol and I finally went to our room and she stripped down naked and sat on her bed, took a cigarette, offered me one, and lighted mine first, looking deep into my eyes. 'You're very attractive, Judy,' she told me after lighting her own cigarette and blowing out the match. 'I bet the boys go for you.' I casually admitted to having dated a few in my time. 'Ever done it with a boy?' she asked directly. 'Not with a boy—a man—and there's some difference!' I announced as if I'd been a woman of the world for years. 'Oh,' was her immediate comment. 'What about you?' I asked. She shrugged, said: 'One boy did it...he was crude.' I asked if she had liked it. 'No,' was her immediate retort. I told her that I'd been lucky to have it with a man who knew how to do a girl. Carol shrugged that off. 'All this boy was interested in was his own satisfaction. I got stuck, but good. I was sick as hell afterwards.' I asked if she'd ever done it again. She said she wouldn't let a guy do it to her again. Then she added: 'You don't need a man to make it!' I laughed at that, said something to the effect that anybody could masturbate, but that it wasn't the same thing. 'I didn't mean it that way.' she announced quite casually. Then she made a switch around, asked: 'Do you like sex—I mean, does it thrill you?' I assured her that I liked it.

'Ever do it with a girl?' The question surprised me for I had never considered the possibility. My lack of knowledge revealed itself immediately with an honest question: 'How the hell can a girl do it to you...? She doesn't have a penis.'

Carol got a kick out of that. For the first time I became conscious of her body. She had lovelier breasts than mine, much larger.

Finally she asked: 'Want to bet a girl doesn't have the equipment to give another girl a thrill?' I was a little high and lonely, and the idea of Larry doing things to my body sent a shiver of excitement through me. I was getting hot enough to fondle with myself. The thought that Carol just might know what she was talking about intrigued me and I shrugged. 'Then get undressed and I'll show you what a woman can do to a woman. I know better than any man knows how to please woman, because I know all those secret places that only another woman could know about.' So I undressed."

"Just like that?"

"Right. Why not? I was inexperienced enough and young enough to be interested in anything sexual." She stubbed out a cigarette and lighted another. "Carol dug my body. She said I had nice breasts and that she wanted to kiss them. Then moving to the light switch at the right of our room's door, she said: 'You just lay back and think of nothing. Just let me show you how it can be. Okay?' I merely nodded, did as told as the light went out.

"The next thing I knew was the sensation of soft lips around one of my breasts. My immediate reaction was that it was difficult to tell the difference between Carol's lips and tongue from that of a boy's.

54

Remember, I'd done a lot of petting and boys had given my breasts a good working over before I met Larry in the bathroom with that thing of his hard as a rock. Then suddenly Carol was all over me, skillfully—very skillfully, I might add. Her hand went across my stomach, lightly touched sensitive areas, then across my thighs, down over my legs, all the time her lips moving from one breast to another. I could feel the points of her breasts brushing my stomach and side every once in a while and it was far from unpleasant. I remember wondering at the time what it might be like to kiss her breasts.

"Then she started fondling me down below, and I was really on fire. How I longed for a man at that moment. I thought of Larry and almost cried out in the agony of not having him. I couldn't imagine what Carol could do to match him. Then suddenly I felt her tongue dip into mine and I started going wild all over. I guess I got an orgasm right off, but she went suddenly wild and' I went wild, gasping, moving on the bed like some big man had taken my body. My arms hit the bed time and time again as Carol kept at me like a fiend. After she seemed to have gotten some pleasure, she sat up, and in the darkness I could just make out a smile on her lips. 'How'd you like it?' she asked. I laughed and said something like what the G-D did she think? Then she asked: 'Would you like to do that to me?' At first the idea sounded shocking, then I realized that it couldn't be any worse than doing it to a man like that, and Larry had always liked to have me on him in that way. I said I'd do my best. She suggested that we make a 69 out of it and I sorta liked *that* idea. Well, we continued on like this for most of the night and I learned what a lesbian affair could be like."

"Which did you like best?"

"Both. Both are different. It's a different kind of experience. I...well, like both very, very much. With a girl you...well...get something that is quite impossible to get with a man—if nothing other than kissing her...breasts."

"Then there have been other girls since then?" I asked.

"Naturally. I made it with Carol all that year—it was some experience."

"Any boy friends during this time?"

"Some. Usually pick-ups. When I got to the point when I absolutely had to have a man I'd pick a cat up. But I always preferred men to boys. Boys were too fast, eager to get into my pants, while men and Carol were gentle and slow, wanting to thrill me as much as I wanted to be thrilled. The boys went at it as if there was a time limit and as if I might disappear before the real goodies had been had. They weren't tender or artful like Larry."

"When did you have a good affair with a boy, if ever?"

"Oh, next summer—at home. I dated some guy and finally when I got to the point where I couldn't stand the playing around, let him have me. He was surprisingly innocent and I had to teach him how to really satisfy a girl. I knew enough about pleasing a man, so I guess he thought I was pretty great. In the end he turned out to be very good."

"You were home at this time?"

"Yes."

"What about Larry?"

"I turned a cold face to him. He accepted it quite casually and that was it."

"Have you ever seen this fellow—the young boy you taught that summer—since?"

"Yes."

"Had intercourse with him."

"No. Never. Once the summer was finished I went back to school."

"Continue your affair with Carol?"

"No."

"What kind of relations did you have during this time?"

"With both boys and girls. I found it easy enough to pick out the girls who liked girls and when there wasn't a boy around I would shack-up with the girls. Some of these girls had apartments away from school, so they could carry on wild parties...and I found my way into these groups. When I got bored I'd go out and pick something up."

"Weren't you afraid of having a baby or catching a social disease?"

"No. Larry had hipped me on what to do. And as you know, I take the pills, so...with the pills and the right shots and keeping myself clean, I can play ball as much as I wish, without any fears."

"What kind of sex do you have, now?"

"At the very moment, nothing—since I'm just sitting here talking to you," she offered with a bright laugh. "And making myself hot all over, and especially down here." She looked pointedly at me.

"I meant, generally."

"I've picked up a pattern. Boys and girls—depending on circumstances, who is around and how I feel."

"Then you still continue having lesbian affairs?"

"I have a girl friend, if that's what you mean—and we do it almost every night I'm home—she lives with me, splitting expenses."

"Doesn't she get a little upset about you going off and having a man?"

"Sure, but that's the arrangement we agreed upon. She has nothing to bitch about. I keep her well satisfied."

"Don't you ever plan on getting married?"

"I guess so...but I can't imagine some guy letting me make it with girls too. Can you?"

"No," I admitted quite honestly. "Don't you want children?"

"Yes...I guess so. But...." She shrugged helplessly.

"Ever wondered why you seek out lesbian affairs?"

"For kicks."

"Why do you like it so much? I mean, there *really* isn't anything that a lesbian can do to you that a man can't. That's a typical homosexual rationalization—and I don't really think of you as being a homosexual—you enjoy it too much with men."

This caused her to become very thoughtful for a long time. As gently as possible I suggested that if she wanted to have children and a normal life, which seemed quite obvious considering her hesitation, that it might be a good idea to think about talking over her problem with somebody who was qualified to offer a solution—one that would give her both sexual satisfaction through the normal relationship between a husband and wife. At first she was a little annoyed by the idea, saying there was nothing wrong with her sexual drives. I said that there was nothing wrong with enjoying sex—and that homosexual relations, while possibly pleasant, were not the ideal norm for the average mature adult person—and that a normal and healthy marriage could not allow homosexual acts. Not to be well balanced. I also pointed out that a true homosexual wasn't a deviant, or pervert, or somebody who could be "cured" but simply a person who has been built to only respond to somebody of the same sex. It was a totally different issue. And I admitted that under some, or even many, circumstances many people could enjoy and respond to homosexual unions, like she apparently did. But that didn't mean they weren't able to live a wonderfully so-called normal life with somebody of the opposite sex.

"A man can do all the things a woman can—and if you remember that, you'll have to accept the idea that possibly you do need professional help to make you able to function in a manner which will not require a lesbian lover. I'm certainly not qualified to help you or even advise you. Only a professional who deals with these kinds of problems every day— who has gone to school to learn his profession— could possible qualify."

She considered this and then, as if irritated by the whole idea announced that it was too difficult to think about it right then and that she was hot for what only I could give her. But after we had made love, she asked, quite suddenly: "Do you really think I should...well...do I need professional help?"

I countered with: "How do you feel about it? Do you think you are able, all alone, by yourself, to straighten things out? I'm assuming you're telling the truth about wanting a husband and children. And you could certainly get both, in time, and adjust to married life—and possibly never seek lesbian love—but you would always wonder, and you would not totally understand yourself the way a professional could give you complete understanding—and without such understanding you will never come to total peace with the problem or yourself. You have a much better chance of finding a rich life with a man who would love you and serve as the total sexual role in your living experience."

COMMENT

The fact is that Judy did seek out good professional help. She learned to understand that her lesbian need had, in part, been caused by guilts brought on by seducing her stepfather, which in turn was caused by a deep-seated hatred for her mother—the kind of hatred brought on by the fact that her mother never had time enough for her when she was growing up. And then there had been the normal jealousy of all the men in her mother's life who had taken away the affection she needed so much.

Her seduction of Larry had partly been caused by a need to "get-even," so to speak. All of which is making her problem seem far simpler than it really was. Nonetheless, Judy did learned to adjust to herself as a total human being and came to terms with her emotional feelings about her mother. She is now married to a man who is quite happy with her, and they have a young daughter upon whom Judy gives the affection she had lacked as a child.

One assumes that her bisexual past is just that done and over with. Even if not, she is now enjoying a far richer living experience through greater understanding of what demons had possessed her in early life. Now, at least, she's in the driver's seat.

Not everybody is as lucky as Judy—not everybody, even with professional help, can find the total adjustment which seems to be hers.

CHAPTER FOUR

Spouse Switchers: Dan and Nancy

Dan is a serious faced young man in his late twenties, his wife, Nancy, is just a couple of years younger with off-blonde hair; neither are what is normally called an outstandingly attractive couple, but there is a clean, middle class look about them—both might be called average. Dan has a slender build and a thin mouth, long nose and a habit of taking his glasses off when making any real serious statement. Nancy is a little nervous and seems, at first, a bit shy and a bit too sweet. If you saw them at a party, or in the normal course of things, you would not guess that they were totally involved and adjusted to the act of swapping partners, commonly called wife swapping or spouse switchers, or even swinging.

"Though," as Dan states a little seriously, "it is not always true that people enjoy it like we do—and we have met many couples falling between twenty-five and thirty-two. Generally this wife-swapping thing is considered as being caused by sexual boredom—a craving for something different and new in ones sex life," he continued the first time we talked about it, at a party where I met them. "This isn't always the case...though with the two of us...I'll be quite frank, we were bored with each other—sounds fantastic, but you have to understand that we were married when we were very young—in our teens. I had just finished high school and she was still attending, and continued while we were still married. We knew nothing much about sex—it was the first time for both of us—while we were still dating." It did not seem to bother him that Nancy was standing there at his side, and she did not seem to mind the drift or honesty of the conversation.

As is the usual pattern, I'll first meet somebody somewhere along the line and, then when they discover what I do for a living and that I've done some books on sex and that I'm always interested in gathering factual material, they will many times open up and start telling me details for which I do not at all ask. In Dan and Nancy's case it became a natural. We arranged a meeting at their home, a small two bedroom house in Tarzana. Drinks were handed out and the conversation was general in the beginning, until Dan asked: "Don't you want to put up your tape recorder?" As I was doing so, he said: "I've always wondered where you birds get your material. I used to think that...well, it couldn't be true. Like us and this wife swapping. It sounds fantastic when I think about it logically."

Nancy, holding a drink between her hands, leaning forward, elbows on her knees, said: "At the time...at first, I mean, it sounded a little disgusting and degrading."

I'd already set the tape recorder into action and

the mike was between the three of us.

"You weren't for it?" I inquired.

Nancy gave me a sweet smile, said: "I didn't even realize it would happen."

"But...how?"

Dan stated, again in that serious manner of his: "I think I might explain. We didn't really know what was going to happen. I mean...I knew that the couples were in the habit of switching with other couples and I was pretty sure what *might* happen, but didn't know *how* it would happen. Nancy here...."

"I just didn't believe that people really acted in that way. I mean, I was brought up in a small town and my parents didn't talk about sex and it was a subject I knew little about. Dan got some of those books—you know about sex—and we read one about wife swapping and I was shocked by the whole idea. Yet, over the weeks and months, after learning that such things took place, I found it sort of interesting. Now, I know, I was actually intrigued by the idea, but unwilling to admit it to myself. And when Dan came home one night and said that his new boss had invited us to dinner and that...well, they were one of those couples who swapped partners, I didn't want anything to do with it."

"She actually went into a rage," Dan explained. "I assured her that this kind of idea was not on my mind and that I knew nothing about his wife and that we had merely been invited over to his house for dinner and that there wasn't anything I could do about it. That the couple were involved in swinging wasn't really a secret—though they didn't put a sign on his office, or have cards printed up saying

'We're Swingers'—but in conversations if matters of a sexual nature happened to pop up or go in the direction of morality, liberal codes of ethics, open marriages, all that kind of thing, well, it became obvious that he was very liberal and quite open to experimental life-styles. In fact, people didn't pick up on this side of his life until having been working for the company for a while. It simply became obvious that he was a very open man about such things. He even had a book in his office on the subject of swinging and wasn't at all hesitant about talking about it. He favored a very liberal life style. Since he owned the company and it did publish a number of books, some on sexuality, well…it all was fairly open without being flaunted. If asked he might tell you; if not, you'd probably never guess. He was neither secretive about their swinging nor did he keep it locked up in the closet. And he never inflicted his ideas on others. So, being asked to dinner to his house was no different from the same request from your average boss. No strings were attached other than one was expected to accept such invitations. This was necessary—a part of my job, you might say. You don't say no to your boss when he offers a dinner. You go on out and have dinner with him. Hank would never inflict his ideals or morality upon others. The fact that he swapped wives with other men had nothing to do with his invitation to dinner.

"Oh, let me correct that some. Hank was not planning on anything sexual—but he was never against it if things worked out that way. Both he and his wife, Ruth, are totally adjusted to switching, but they don't go about forcing awkward situations Like Hank told me once, 'There are enough couples who play the game our way, so we don't have to go about introducing other couples into the action.' This statement, we've learned since, is quite true."

Nancy nodded. "Hank is almost fanatical about that. Even the first time he said it wasn't necessary that I do it with him—that was when we were alone in one of the bedrooms. He was very nice about it all, He seemed to sense my own hesitation and fears. He didn't believe that anybody should be forced to do anything sexual against their wills. He believes simply that sex is a part of a human's normal nature and that it is either totally fed or it is submerged in fears and guilts and...well, he did a lot to straighten me out." Nancy looked at her husband and smiled tenderly.

"To be truthful," Dan told me, taking off his glasses, "I didn't know what to expect. I'd learned from Hank that he *had,* at times, tried the switching game—but only with people who actually wanted the same thing. I'd been told by one of the other office guys—who had been invited to his place the weekend before—that nothing even subtly suggestive or different had gone on—it had been just a nice social dinner with drinks before and afterwards. Just sort of getting to know each other. Sam said that his wife would never go in for that sort of thing and neither would he."

"I was scared," Nancy admitted, after taking a sip of her drink, "but there just wasn't anything we could do."

I asked: "How did it happen?"

"In the beginning," Dan told me, "the evening progressed quite naturally as any would. A couple of social cocktails, a nice dinner—roast and baked

66

potatoes. Ruth was dressed in a red cocktail gown that did nice things to her voluptuous figure. She is about five years older than me. Several times I saw her eyes, very large and deep brown, glancing in my direction. But I guess I was fairly much on the alert for any suggestion of...well, anything different. After dinner Nancy worked on the dishes and Hank and I went into the study.

"Hank merely said: 'You have a very attractive wife.' I returned the compliment. Then I added: 'How can you stand the idea...well of other guys....' And he finished it with a smile and a bold: 'Making love to her?' I nodded and he said this: 'I love my wife and I want her to have all the pleasure in the world—I want to give her everything possible—and we have discovered that in our relationship that it helps our own love-making to have experienced sexual pleasure with others. You learn new things—you discover greater love for one another—you are put in a position where experimentation takes place. And most important of all, you learn the difference between pure sexual pleasure and sexual-love pleasure. There is a difference.

"Because I love Ruth I want her to have all the pleasure possible; it does not bother me that another man can give her physical orgasm—she *loves* me. I know that and she knows it—and that's enough for both of us. She enjoys talking to other people—so I should be jealous that she gets this kind of mental pleasure from others? The logical extension is that—I shouldn't let it bother me that she gets sexual pleasure from another man—just so that she always comes back to me and wants me above all others. That's the kicker.'

"This all surprised me," Dan continued, "Because I had never thought of it in that manner. But when he put it that way...I could see the logic in the thing. And I'll admit, Ruth was a very attractive woman and it was just natural for a man to wonder what it would be like with her. Doing something about it was something totally different."

Nancy put in at this point: "I had insisted on helping Ruth with the dishes and she allowed me to talk her into it. I know now that I wanted to be alone with her and that she sensed this. Ruth told me, much later, that this is one of the patterns. They have gotten to recognize couples who are intrigued with the idea of swapping—and they will roll with the punches. If nothing is offered—fine, they've had a lovely social evening. That's that. Well, while we were doing the dishes, I kept wanting to ask Ruth about this swapping thing—but I didn't really admit it quite so boldly to myself. Finally she said, pausing long enough to look into my eyes: 'You've been wondering about us, haven't you?' There wasn't anything I could really say about that. I merely looked down at the floor. She laughed gently, then asked: 'How long have you been married to your husband?'

"There was something about the way she accented the last two words which caused me to realize that she accepted Dan as my own personal property and would never think of interfering with this...well, what would you call it—relationship between Dan and me—no matter what. I know now that it was exactly what she was trying to put across. She was saying in effect that even if we did swap husbands for the night it would be only for the night and that Dan was mine, no matter what might go on between him and her. By implication I received the message that Hank was totally hers, no matter what. I told her that I'd been seventeen when I married Dan and that I'd never had anybody else before him or after him. That last just popped out and I was immediately embarrassed. She told me, 'It was the same with Hank and me, though we were a little older at the time we married. I wouldn't let him go to bed with me until we were married, though we did much of what leads up to intercourse.'

"Her manner of speaking about sex was so natural that I found that the embarrassment just slipped away and I felt for the first time in life almost freed from the emotional and mental guilt I'd always felt about sex. Here was a woman who was far more experienced than me, and I reasoned unshockable. 'Dan is a good lover...at least I think so...but we knew nothing about sex when we got married, and...well, I've always wondered what another man might be like. I'd never dream of....'

"At this point I stopped talking because what I had been about to say, I realized, was not the truth. After a moment's thought, while Ruth wisely waited in silence, I continued: "I had never dreamed about actually having an affair with a man...another man...because I love Dan too much to do such a thing to him. I couldn't cheat on him.'

Ruth smiled, and then continued with the dishes, handing them to me to dry, all the time talking, saying things like: 'That's the real explanation, at least for me, to your first question, Nancy. I'd always wondered, but fought the questions down.

"Then one night we met a couple and...well,

things just developed rather naturally—and they told us that they had done some swapping and that it had made their lives far happier—that they had learned to adjust to themselves better as sexual partners. We had been drinking and...I really can't remember exactly how it all happened so fast, but suddenly we had made the decision and I was in a bedroom with this other man and he made love to me, very good, too. I was surprised how good he was—yet, at the same time, how much more I liked it with Hank. The difference is quite simply that sex by itself can be lovely and exciting and pleasant, but with love mixed in, it is far better.

"The next time I slept with Hank we were both anxious to try some of the new little subtle things we had learned from the swapping. From that moment on our sexual relations have been far better than we could have imagined possible before starting the swapping. Everybody has their own little pattern, and to learn about that pattern is to break your own, and to change your own. You grow from experience, and it does not change your love for your husband.' By the time we had finished the dishes there was an automatic agreement that this evening the four of us would be changing partners. Ruth did not ask it in words and I don't think I could have given my consent, verbally, but the conversation just developed and there was no questioning about the fact that each of us would sleep with the other's husband."

"Just as simple as that?" I asked, a little surprised, both at the young woman's bold statement and the fact that she could talk so openly about it.

"Just that simple," she assured me. "By the time

70

the dishes were finished the two of us were agreed—silently—upon what would happen.

"I didn't know how it would take place—but I was a willing student and Ruth a good teacher."

Dan smiled and said: "I was more startled than you can imagine. It was just about the last thing I ever expected to happen. Hank and me were now talking about the political state of affairs and when Ruth and Nancy joined us, my mind was far away from wife swapping. Ruth just walked up to me, said: 'You have a darling wife, Dan, we had a wonderful conversation. Now it's our turn to get to know one another better.' The way she took hold of my arm was warm, intimate and aggressive. I glanced at Nancy, horrified that she would think what I was thinking. I could just imagine her reaction to Ruth's rather suggestive, bold actions and words, But after a quick, warm smile, Nancy moved to Hank, and said something to the effect that Ruth was really wonderful and that he was lucky to have a wife who loved him so much."

Nancy laughed. "You should have seen the startled expression on Dan's face. He didn't know what to do. I'd watched Ruth, let her enter the room first, to see what she did—and when she made her move to Dan, I knew she was leading the way, showing me how to handle the situation —letting me know how to play the game. All I could think of was trying to make it...well, to be honest, I was scared to death of making a fool of myself. I simply followed Ruth's lead—twisting it around. The rest was up to Hank, and he knew how to handle it. Instead of making a direct, aggressive move, he suggested cocktails and taking my arm, asked if I might like to help him make them up."

"That," Dan stated, "left Ruth and me alone in the den, while Nancy and Hank went into the kitchen. Ruth was very quick to say: 'We had a nice conversation, Dan. We understand each other, and your wife understands that you are hers and I'm Hank's and that nothing can change that.' I mumbled something awkward and Ruth merely laughed. Then I asked: 'What the hell did you talk about?'

"Her answer startled me for it was so direct that it took my breath away, 'About love and husbands and wives—and to be quite honest, about swapping mates. She was really very interested and came right out and asked me—though subtly. I reassured her that nobody could come between me and Hank and that I was not the kind of woman to even attempt to touch another woman's husband without her consent—though I went about it subtly. We understand each other, Dan—and she is the type of woman who could never cheat on her husband. She loves you very much—but I could see right at the beginning that she is a normal, healthy young woman—and women are much like men when it comes to sexual drives. A woman sometimes wonders about men like men wonder about other women.'

"She went on like that for some time, totally convincing me that Nancy was agreeable to swapping and that it would actually help our own personal sex life—saying much of what Nancy told you Ruth said to her."

"What was Hank saying to you?" I asked Nancy.

"Nothing. He merely mixed the drinks, talked about how much he liked my husband. He didn't make any passes, didn't do anything suggestive. Though, in fact, the arrangement had already been made, we had *already* switched partners. I sat there wondering what it would be like with Hank, and realized that it wouldn't be long before I would find out. The idea fascinated me. I kept wondering if he was as large as Dan. Things like that. It didn't occur to me to wonder what he might do that was different. I was curious about the size of him. Funny what a person thinks at a time like that. Maybe a little afraid...I didn't want to be hurt, or anything like that."

"When," I asked, "did the actual splitting up take place?"

Dan took up the conversational ball at this point. "They returned to the den with drinks, we talked, Ruth at my side, Nancy at Hank's. The conversation was general and social. We finished the drinks and then Ruth said, in the manner which most women will use at parties—though meaning something totally different, like mind if I dance with your husband, or have conversation with him...something innocent like that: 'Mind if I borrow your husband for a moment, Nancy?' The hairs at the back of my head prickled. I stared at Nancy, wondering what her reaction would be. This was, in actual fact, the moment of truth. Either we backed down now—and we could and that would have been it—or we continued all the way through."

"I knew," Nancy put in, "what must be going on inside Dan's mind and wanted desperately to tell him it was all right. When Ruth actually asked my permission, in this subtle manner, I realized we had an out. I didn't hesitate a moment in saying: 'Of course not, Ruth. I have Hank here to keep me company.' It was a silly remark, but it made the point quite clear to Dan—and hopefully relieved his mind."

I asked: "What happened then?"

"Ruth took hold of my arm and then laughingly waved Hank and Nancy good-bye and led me across the living room, into the hall and to one of the bedrooms. She closed the door behind us and then turned toward me, looking up into my eyes. I could see the crevice between her breasts and found myself already beginning to react to both her and the situation. She slipped her arms around my neck and gently kissed me on the lips. Her body was soft and her breasts pressed against me, yieldingly. Her hips slipped back and forth and I felt her thigh move between my legs."

At this point, Nancy stood said there was something she had to take care of and left us. Dan grinned. "Nancy wants me to tell you all you need to know—but doesn't want to be embarrassed by it. We arranged that. When I've finished she'll come in and tell her story—I'll leave then."

I nodded, said: "Continue."

"I was getting already stiff as a rock. Ruth felt the hardness with her thigh and then slipped back, away from me. Her right hand reached out and caressed what was like a long rock against my shorts. 'You do find me exciting. That's nice.' She touched me again and then said that it might be better if we got undressed, unless I wanted to undress her. I shrugged and watched as she reached around to her back and unzipped the dress which fell to puddle about her feet.

"She stood there in a black half-bra, which exposed the tips of her nipples and black garter belt that held up smooth nylon stockings. The sight was highly stimulating. She was a beautifully shaped woman. Her breasts are larger than Nancy's, her hips wider. Those legs, encased in the stockings, were full, lovely and very exciting to look at.

"'Get undressed, honey,' she instructed me, while starting to remove her bra. Those breasts burst outwards, but didn't seem to drop very much. They were full and supple, far more shapely than I would have imagined possible, considering their size. I was shaking as I started to undress. I watched her unlatch her stockings from the garter belt and then slip them slowly down over her long legs. She made quite a show of it and seemed to enjoy my watching her undress. She looked up into my eyes every now and then to be sure I was watching. As she removed the garter belt, I was peeling off my shirt. As the garter belt fell to the floor I was beginning to unbuckle my pants with shaking hands. She stood there before me in see——-through, lacy black panties—those bikini type panties, very small. 'Want me to take them off?' she asked, touching the panties. I shook my head and she merely nodded and stepped close as I slipped out of my slacks. Her right hand reached out and slid under my jocks, pulled them down and exposed me.

"'My,' she said, 'you certainly are well endowed.' I countered with: 'What'd you expect after that little display?' She laughed throatily, fondled me, squeezing and caressing. Her fingers played with the tip and then searched down lower, handling me with expert care. Her hand patted my balls, very tenderly, then helped me finish undressing, caressing my body as if it was something beautiful. Then she came into my arms, soft and hot, breasts throbbing up and down against me. We frenched. We kept that up until my hard was just guided against her luscious honey pot. I warned her to not move too much or else I wouldn't be able to hold back. Her laughter was filled with delight. She withdrew from me, stood back a step, hands on hips. 'Why don't you take off my panties?' I moved forward and started to do exactly what she suggested. Then she grabbed hold of my right hand and placed it where it would do both of us the most good. 'Just enjoy yourself, Dan. Do what comes naturally. You can do anything you want to me. There isn't anything I don't go for.'

"My hand was trembling as it lay there on her most intimate part. Then she reached out and grabbed hold of me like she'd done before. I guess I sort of went wild and when she released her hold I fell to my knees before her and buried my face against her, lips and tongue going mad. She moaned and then said something about transferring to the bed. Somehow we got onto the bed and when I started to continue what I'd been doing, Ruth shifted around so that her mouth was placed directly over my...well it was damned hard, I can tell you... throbbing hard...hurting hard. It was the first time anything like this had happened to me and I went out of my mind. The two of us feasted greedily upon one another, then the lights went out. Later we did it the conventional way."

"Didn't you feel any guilt about making love to Ruth?"

"Why?"

"Well, Nancy seemed to have gone along with the idea and it wasn't cheating. I remembered what Hank had told me about loving your wife enough to want her to have as much pleasure as possible and I only hoped he was good and gentle enough to her to give her pleasure. I was fairly sure he would be."

"What happened afterwards?"

"We got dressed and went into the den to have a drink, Hank was there, sipping whiskey, and said that Nancy was sleeping. Later, after several drinks I went in and woke Nancy and we went home, after she got dressed."

"Didn't the two of you feel strange—I mean…."

"Well, we were silent all the way home. When we went to bed she came into my arms like a little child and we made tender love. Afterwards we talked about it and learned that it didn't change anything about our feelings towards one another. If anything, we loved one another all the more—or, to put it another way: we understood the fullness of our love, and that it wasn't just sexual desire, but something far more meaningful."

"Had Hank been…?"

"Good to Nancy? I think she can tell you best." We called Nancy in and Dan left. I came directly to the point. "What happened after Ruth and Dan left you with Hank?"

"We talked, finished our drinks and he offered me another, which I was very thankful for. He didn't push matters and knew to take things easy. Once I was beginning to feel my drinks, he took my hand in his, said: 'Nancy, you are a very beautiful and desirable woman.' That was all. I followed him into a bedroom, across the house from the one in which Ruth had taken Dan.

"We closed the door behind us and like I said, Hank offered me an out, but I didn't take it. He then pulled me gently into his arms and kissed my lips, very tenderly. He was gentle and tender. I was excited, flush with drinks and...a little frightened, too. But all I could think of was finding out if he was like Dan. Funny thing is that I never really found out that night. He turned off the lights and then reached for me in the darkness, pulling my body close, covering my lips with first gentle, then passionate kisses. His hands moved about my back, seeming to have electric fire in them. I was getting so excited that I could hardly think—it was even hard to breathe and I was mentally screaming to be out of my clothes in order to breathe more easily. His hand covered my breast, fondling gently, then he slipped a caressing hand down over my hip, then between them for a moment and it felt good. Then Hank, with great gentleness, led me to the bed, then started to undress me. He was so skillful at it that I was only aware of his hands, which seemed to be caressing and caressing.

"My breasts were tight knots, burning with fire and every time his hand touched them, I wanted to fairly scream in the pleasure of it. When he touched me more intimately I could hardly control myself. By the time I was stripped naked, he had worked me up so much that I could think of nothing other than getting him in me—it was as simple at that, I wanted to have the pressure and pain relieved. He started stripping and then once he was naked, standing before me—I sat on the edge of the bed during this time—I leaned forward and kissed him there. It was the first time that the idea of worshipping a man's...well—"

"Penis?"

"Yes." Her face flushed for a moment and then she shook her head. "Silly to get all worked up over just one word. Well, I'd never thought to worship a man in that way. But I was excited and I would have worshipped anything that would relieve my excitement....

"In the end we were both pulsating against one another in perfect union and when he finally stiffened for the last time I felt a multiple, convulsive pleasure and fell back against the bed, totally exhausted. The next thing I knew was Dan kissing me. It was very nice, very pleasant to wake to Dan's kissing. I couldn't wait to get home and see if he would make love to me. I wanted him so much, I wanted to know that things hadn't changed, and wanted so very much to be reassured that he still desired me after having...well, sex with Ruth. It was great." She hesitated, then smiled shyly. "I really don't want to talk about what happened to Dan and me. That's private—our personal business. But....

"I'll say this one thing, I've learned to totally understand my love for Dan—and we have grown closer together since then. Every time we swap, we end up making love to each other in new and exciting ways—right after we get home. It was one habit we have kept to. I've seen men who are stronger, bigger, hairy, even maybe better lovers than Dan— but none who give me the emotional and Spiritual satisfaction which giving myself to my husband brings to me. It isn't even important if I have an orgasm with Dan—though that is one thing I've been very lucky about with him —for just the act of giving myself to my husband and giving him pleasure is enough in itself."

COMMENT

Dan returned a short time after that and we talked generally about many topics. The subject of sex didn't come up again during the evening, other than one footnote: I asked if they were happy with their arrangement. The expression both gave each other was so totally filled with love and tender understanding that I knew it was out of the question to suggest that their swapping was, to say the least, a little progressive for most people—and that maybe they might find greater happiness in learning to correct this habit.

To me, personally, the relationship between a man and woman—husband and wife—should be total—and it should be personal and intimate and selfish in that it is not shared with any outsider. But perhaps it is better to swap wives openly than cheat on one another secretly. I could not, personally, function in such a manner as Dan and Nancy do. For them it seems to be their answer to happiness—and they aren't going out and trying to change others to their way of life—only seeking those willing to cooperate. It is their answer to happiness; not mine. And somehow I can't help thinking they are missing out on something more beautiful—the ability to love one another totally and with full understanding, without the necessity of comparing each other with strangers—without the necessity of searching new by-ways to sexual pleasure through wife swapping. The people who can adjust without such drastic measures as Dan and Nancy, Hank and Ruth, are, I believe, far better off, far better adjusted to life and themselves and each other. But if it works, as with them it obviously does, don't rock the boat. I believe that if they were to seek professional advice they would learn that it is possible to find total satisfaction with one another without the necessity of using the changing partners game as a sexual or emotional crutch to understanding. To me their answer is not an ideal one—only more honest, and healthier than cheating behind each other's back. Not all wife-swapping is done in such a manner; not all is so well adjusted and usually will cause deep-seated emotional problems between the couple which neither realize as being caused by their sexual looseness.

Most important is the fact that many marriages have been demolished as a result of swinging. It is almost an exception to find people like Dan and Nancy who have discovered it to be a solution to their needs. Some couples end up trying it for a while, then drift away. There are many life-styles, some that actually work for those involved in them, many are nothing more than momentary experiments which have good and bad effects on their lives.

For the average person swinging is not a solution to any marital or sexual problem, and while it might resolve normal questions as to "wonder what its like with another partner" it can all too often be the beginning of the end of a marriage that might have resolved its differences through professional help of a trained therapist. Of course, many marriages which are on the rocks to begin with may find themselves experimenting in swinging as a bridge to divorce.

We all seek a better life, and we all seek to grow. Some methods are healthy, others damning and dangerous.

That, in the long run, is the only moral conclusion one can come to.

Not a matter of right and wrong, but merely a matter of what ultimately brings about a successful relationship and happiness.

I tend to believe that honest communication and hard work is a part of the marriage pack, and only in a mutual effort to work things out to each other's satisfaction do we have any chance at discovering happiness.

For some the solution is swinging. And one can't condemn success.

CHAPTER FIVE

The Competing Mother: Helen

When I met Helen, she was drunk in the way only a thirty-five-year-old, attractive, and sexy woman can be drunk: slobby, sexy and feeling depressed and low. I had known "another" Helen a few years back, but the woman I met this afternoon was totally different from the one she had been before. We had been good friends during our first encounter—though strangely enough no sexual affair had developed. I hadn't heard from Helen once during all this time, then suddenly she called me on the phone, said that she needed somebody to talk to. I invited her over, told her how to get to my place and then set aside the manuscript I'd been working on, pulled out a bottle of whiskey and waited.

Helen arrived half an hour after she hung up the phone, sloppy drunk. Once I'd closed the door behind her, she stood leaning against the door, hips thrust out. She is a highly developed woman with a sensual mouth, angular features, but actually not very tall, just topping five feet four; though gives the impression of being classically voluptuous and big.

She looked at me, then threw her arms about my neck. "Oh, it's good to see you," she slobbered. Then after a quick kiss stepped back, said: "You know, I've often wondered why we never made it in bed together."

Interestingly enough she wasn't slurring her words. She spoke quite fluidly.

I merely shrugged, then offered her a drink I was sure she didn't need. I was surprised by the lack of physical change in Helen. Only her eyes revealed any change; they seemed haunted. She sat on the sofa, her legs crossed, skirt high. After sipping her drink, she looked into my eyes, said:

"Would it shock you if I said I need a little loving...well, a man...Christ, just a damned screw job?"

I gaped at her, not quite shocked, but a little surprised. We always had been able to talk fairly boldly about ourselves and our private lives, but the expression on her face had made the statement quite personal. She needed a man, and I was a man, and I could do something about it if...I would.

"What is it?" I inquired, trying to change the direction of her thoughts.

"Not right now. I want to talk. We've known each other long enough to be honest. Hell, we've known each other long enough to have screwed each other a thousand times. Not literally, of course. But...I've always wondered...."

The brazen words seemed to delight her, dropping from that sensual full mouth so casually that it seemed almost natural. Yet she had never seemed a down right vulgar woman.

"What is it you want, Helen?" I inquired, still trying to keep my cool.

"Right now I wasn't thinking of conversation. You always did find me attractive, didn't you?"

"Any man would," I admitted calmly.

"Then hell. We're big boys and girls. Wanna piece of action, feller?" She laughed, stood and lifted up her skirt.

Her words and action were designed to entice, exciting a male in the most blunt manner—not being "ladylike" nor attempting to leave any doubt as to what she wanted. Of course, verbal invitation was hardly needed. Yet, for some reason, she felt the need to come on very strong, much more like a man than a woman. She'd always been outspoken, but never quite this blunt nor forward. Of course, considering our "history" which had been somewhat non-sexual, at least in practice, her actions were without hesitation nor embarrassment, but rather strongly seductive, to say the least. She was leaving nothing to the imagination.

There wasn't anything on underneath and there wasn't any restrain from that moment on between either of us.

Afterwards, Helen sat smoking, nude, on the sofa, fingering her glass of whiskey and seven-up. It was a long time before she began speaking. A lot of things were said which were general and pointless, but finally her voice lowered. "You know my daughter, Karen. She's quite a big girl now, eighteen. I can hardly believe it—but, I was seventeen when I had her."

I remembered Karen. Even at fifteen the girl had been attractive and desirable; loveable. "Popular with the boys?"

Helen nodded and then spat out: "That's the trouble. That's what I've got to talk to somebody about—and it looks like you're elected." She seemed almost sober.

For a short time the conversation drifted and I let Helen take the controls, leading the subject matter back to where she wanted it, when she was ready to speak. We talked about my work, I mentioned the book I was doing about driven deviates and she said that her story might fit and that I was welcomed to it, just so that I kept her real identity out of it.

Once the tape recorder was in place, Helen had lighted another cigarette. It was some time, and half a reel of tape later, before she brought up the subject she had come to talk about.

"It's Karen and her boy friends and me. That sounds a little wild, but...I better start from the beginning, so to speak. I remember you saying something about stories having a beginning, middle and end. There isn't any end, but there's a beginning and I'm right in the middle of it right now...and it is a dilly."

She had more to drink and then continued.

"One day, oh, about six months ago, Karen came home with a young man, about twenty-two, good looking and muscular as hell. I'd been high and dry for months; no current boy friends. I was unhappy and depressed. It was Saturday and I'd fixed an early afternoon drink. I offered Karen and her date—we'll call him Bill—a drink, which they both took willingly enough. Karen was dressed in a sweater and skirt which showed off her figure pretty nicely. I was dressed in a full skirt and a loose blouse, but somehow—and I think I'd done it unconsciously—the top buttons of my blouse were open and gave a nice breasty view, which I noticed Karen's date kept looking at. I learned that he was one of those sports fanatics—captain of his team and all that.

"I suddenly realized that here was a stud who was drinking with two attractive women and finding his attention split between them. It was the first time that I actually accepted my daughter as a woman in a conscious way—I mean as a *woman* with whom I had to compete for men's attention. I was automatically, without desiring it, competing with her right then.

"He had made the situation develop, in that he found me interesting enough to keep giving me side-long glances. I leaned over our home bar, so that my breasts were half laying on the top, in full view of this big husky, muscular sexual animal. I felt dirty and excited and wanted a man like hell. When Karen went to the john, things developed fast! When she had left, Bill said: 'I thought your daughter was great—but never imagined that her mother would be so young and beautiful.'

"His direct play was that of a young man out to get the action where it fell. He hadn't been fooled by my casualness, and as far as he was concerned, my subtle offering of a view of my breasts had been the same as saying let's go into the corner and screw. And in fact that was exactly what I wanted so bad that I hurt where it hurts a girl most.

"Instead of playing the shocked mother, or attempting to direct his attention elsewhere, I merely smiled and said: 'That's a very nice thing to say. I would imagine you've known a lot of girls in your day.' He grinned wolfishly and let his eyes linger on my breasts. 'I've had a few in my time, but never known one as attractive and mature as you are.' Realizing that Karen would be back soon and knowing that nothing in the world could happen this afternoon, I said rather casually, 'You know, Bill, there are girls and there are women. Women know what life's all about. You get my meaning?' He nodded, then said: 'When and where?' Without even batting an eye, I told him I would be at Sam's Bar the next afternoon at one and then quickly changed the topic of conversation as Karen stepped into the room.

"I'll tell you this much, I went through hell the rest of the day and night and the next morning. I kept telling myself I wouldn't do it, and that it was dirty and sick. I kept telling myself all the way to Sam's bar the next day. I just went out for a walk about twelve-thirty and went directly towards Sam, I didn't pass go or anything and I didn't collect any two hundred dollars." She laughed at this old joke and then shrugged. "When I found myself sitting on a barstool in Sam's, I was a little shocked, because I didn't remember anything from the time I left the house to the moment I was conscious of holding a drink in my hands at the bar. Immediately I started to get up, but a hand covered my right shoulder, a voice said: 'Hi, I was afraid you were putting me on, yesterday.'

"A sense of wild relief shot through me. It was out of my hands. A thrilling wave of excitement was already attacking my body at the physical contact of that large hand on my shoulder. He sat down beside me, ordered a beer, and managed to place his right thigh against mine.

"All at once it was so exciting. I thought, here was a young guy, one of my daughter's boy friends, and he was going to give it to me in a short time. I just couldn't wait and said something to the effect that it might be better if we leave. He grinned, downed his beer almost in one gulp and then escorted me out of the bar, holding my elbow with strong fingers.

"His car was painted a violent purple and he drove like his tail was on fire. I almost had a heart attack—but found it thrilling and exciting. He drove out into the countryside and then went down a small road for about a mile, turned left along a dirt road. Parking the car a few hundred feet in front of a small brook, he got out, opened the trunk, grabbed a blanket and then shouted, 'What the hell are you waiting for, an invitation?' He expected me to get out on my own, and I accepted this automatically.

"We walked to the brook, and he spread the blanket out under a tree, took off his shirt and then his T-shirt. I was blown away by the sight of his young strong muscles. He had shoulder, arm, chest and stomach muscles like Mr. U.S.A., and all I could think of was the most important muscle of all and how big and strong it would be. Sorta scary, that. He glared at me as if something was wrong, then said, 'Look, I'm not expecting you to strip me—I expect the same from you. Undress...so I can see those big tits of yours.'

"I shrugged, got a charge watching him step out of his jeans. He was wearing a very brief pair of shorts and I could see from the way they swelled out that he was big enough for two of me. I made no efforts to make a project number out of getting stripped to the waist. He gaped at my breasts and said, 'Mother, do you got them large as melons. You're gonna be just great.'

"He was a bit crude, somewhat...well, not very mature in the manner, certainly not sophisticated or anything like that. And in a strange way that was somewhat exciting. Not Mr. Smooth at all. But... frankly? He was a real turn on.

"His shorts seemed to grow smaller against him and I could hardly keep from laughing in delight. I stripped down to my panties and then stepped toward him, placing my hands on his large, swelling shoulder muscles. 'You are strong, so strong and hard.' He laughed, said: 'Wait until you discover the main attraction.' I boldly reached down and felt the star of the show and it made his shoulder muscles seem like putty. He was taken by surprise by the move and I realized for the first time that he had probably never had it with a real mature woman and that his bold, commanding act had been a cover-up. Now I felt a greater strength than all the muscular power in his shoulders. I would be the seducer—total and bold. I would be teaching the man...okay, boy—male! I took hold of him and then pulled down his shorts. He was amazed by my boldness, but attempted to act as if he knew exactly what was going on and as if it were happening to him this way every day of his life. When I slipped down onto my knees and started worshipping what was going to give me such total pleasure before the afternoon was finished, he gasped out in surprise and seemed to go emotionally limp—as if overwhelmed by what I was doing to him.

90

"How strong and muscular he was, how wonderful and beautiful his body. His chest was covered with dark curly hair which I enjoyed rubbing my breasts against. By the time I'd played my little aggressive game on him, using every trick I knew, he was almost beyond the point of controlling what comes naturally and I was already so hot and hurting it was impossible to keep from wanting. I wanted to feel the total pleasure of knowing his main event grinding away at my hips. I couldn't wait, and I knew he couldn't, so I simply said: 'Now, lover, come down and give me all you have.'

"I lay on my back offering the target for his steel lance which moved quickly into place, bringing such a sensation of voluptuous pleasure that I went wild right at the beginning. He was young and strong and, even for his lack of experience, able to last fairly long. When it was over, I was hardly turned on—oh, I got the goodies, real good, I might add—but I wanted more and more. I was turned on like never before. This was something wild and exciting and overwhelming. He fell on his back, laying there, momentarily satisfied, but I reached for him, and started doing things to him with my mouth and tongue and finally feasted upon his main attraction until it got big enough to enjoy my body again. This time I straddled him and controlled the motions and it lasted a much longer time.

"Afterwards we lighted cigarettes and then teased each other with intimate caresses. By the time the cigarettes were finished we were ready. If he was pleased and surprised by my open boldness and mature sexual experience, I was almost shocked by his ability to go on and on. We did everything I could think of and then some. It was dark by the time we had finished with one another—and when I say finished, I mean that totally. We'd exhausted every possible sexual situation—even at one point where he turned me over his legs and spanked the hell out of my bottom until I got orgasm just because of that. I was totally overwhelmed by his power and strength and sexual energy—he was, in turn, I guess, overjoyed to have a woman who went in for everything. I guess it taught him a lot about sex and women. And it taught me a lot about young men—and the thrill of teaching...and taking the young boyfriends away from my daughter. That was the greatest thing about it, I guess. I've found it that way every time."

"With him, you mean?" I inquired.

She shook her head angrily. "Never more than once with any one boy friend. But I've been going after each of her boy friends keeping damned sure they are over twenty-one—you know that thing about seducing someone underage...." Her voice drifted away and she lighted another cigarette with shaking hands.

"Every time I felt disgusted with myself afterwards, but was unable to control the urge. The guys my own age...well, they can be great for a bed session—but they...well, it's just different. Some of the young ones go off right away and I have one hell of a time getting them excited again. Some are awkward and don't even know what to do with a girl. Some know the score and just lay back and learn more about sex from a woman willing to teach them. Later I feel dirty and guilty and like hell—and I'll get drunk to blindness. Karen doesn't know. At least I don't believe she does, because she has never indicated, but how long can it continue like this without her finding out and what do I do then? The responsibilities of being a mother...oh, hell," she cried, tears streaming down her cheeks, "I just don't know what to do!"

After a moment she shook her head, wiped away the tears, looked at me, smiled gently. "You know I'm not a tramp. But...I've been acting more like a tramp than anything else these last months. I've had to talk to somebody about it. I don't know what makes me be this way and...."

"I think you do know, Helen," I stated in a level, serious voice.

"But I don't!" she cried, alarmed.

"You have a young beautiful daughter, dating attractive men—you are still beautiful and attractive and have the experience which your daughter lacks, and this alone makes you a far more rewarding experience for a man than she would be. You can give mature love and understanding to a sexual relationship—but you aren't even attempting this. Instead of seeking a normal love affair with a man your own age, you are competing with your daughter—because of that age old reason too common to point out."

Slowly she nodded. "I guess you're right about that. I am competing with her. And saying it in that manner makes it sound so damned foolish. It is true that a mature man can give so much more to a relationship of this kind than some young boy.... I feel so damned cheap and dirty."

COMMENT

When I suggested a professional friend of mine to Helen, she immediately agreed to an interview. It took very little time to straighten Helen out, simply because she had already recognized the reasons why she had willfully gone about seducing her daughter's boy friends. Too many mothers feel resentment towards their daughters as they grow older. As the mother realizes that the daughter is no longer a child, a complex of emotional problems will well up in the older woman, made more difficult to bear because many times, as with Helen, the mother is entering the change of life. Helen needed to be reassured that she was still sexually desirable, but went about it in a very childish, immature manner. Luckily for her and her daughter, Karen never found out the truth. Their relationship now is good, according to the last letter I received from Helen—and this is one jump on most mother/daughter relationships. Too many mothers have a little of Helen in them and let this "Helen" complex blind out the natural mother love, to depress it into a distorted horrible thing. Very few will go as far as Helen did—but what is far sadder is that even less will recognize the problem for what it is and get professional help; thus learning to deal with it. In Helen's case one must say that in the end things worked out right, and they became far more adjusted than most such relationships between daughter and mother.

CHAPTER SIX

Paul and June—a Strange Pair

Paul is a sad-faced young man in his late twenties, slight of build and highly nervous, smoking one cigarette after another. He had black wavy hair and rather thin lips, a long straight nose and deep-set eyes. He likes to talk about sex and seems to delight in hearing about sex. We met through a mutual friend several months before the taping. Since June is very important to his story, it is necessary to say something about her, June is highly attractive, with a willowy figure and small breasts. She doesn't top much above five feet and is dark haired and dark eyed, with full attractive lips. To set the stage for her entrance it might be wise to state that Paul had said, during the tape interview, he might send his wife over to me.

I was sitting watching television one evening when the front door bell rang and when I opened it to find this lovely, slender, flashing-eyed woman standing there, I was startled, for I had never met her.

She said almost immediately: "I'm Paul's wife.

He said to come over. I guess you know why."

Before I could say anything, she had pushed her way into the apartment, coming to a stance in the middle of the room. She eyed me in a very challenging way, hands on hips, lips curled up in blatant interest. "He said there was a favor to repay—but didn't say who owed the favor. Why don't you close the door and bring out a drink. I'm thirsty."

She sat on the sofa as I moved into the kitchen, a little startled by her entrance and knowing exactly what she had in mind. I'd never met anybody quite like her—yet it fell true to form, according to Paul's own story.

She was wearing capris and a sweater when I entered the kitchen, nothing when I returned.

She laughed at the shocked expression on my face. "I feel I know you, Carson," she announced. "Paul told me about you and about the books you write and about the fact that he told you the story of our lives together—so don't be so shocked. I came over for a piece of the action, so to speak. I'm horny, tonight. Paul didn't what to do anything—I could have gone out and picked up some guy or... well, he said you wouldn't mind."

The fact was that I minded very much. But I sat down beside her, trying hard to keep my eyes away from her pert little breasts, whose nipples were already hardening into tiny points. Her legs were crossed so that it was impossible to see much more than black curly fleece.

She took the drink and then touched my cheek. "I guess you think I'm something of a kook."

"Well, yes...it is rather startling to have a strange girl step into your apartment and strip down bare."

"Paul told you that I didn't like playing about the bush. I always went after what I wanted. I go after men when they burn my pants. Paul says I have hot pants for any dick on the street. Maybe he's right."

Her talk was a little crude under the circumstances, but I managed to ignore it. "Then you like the arrangement the two of you have?"

"Listen, friend. I dig it the most. I've always been stud-happy. When I was a teenager I put out to all the boys at school who wanted me. In college I had a session with half a dozen guys at once. That was great for kicks. Real crazy. I'm just over-sexed, that's the beginning of the end of it. That was good. I like every kind of sexual situation. I like men— Paul wanted to marry me, so...so, I lay down the law. If he wanted me, it would be under my conditions. I'd been swinging loose all my life and wanted to continue. I used to tease him when we were dating and sexing it up, by telling him about my other men. He seemed to like that. It all worked out pretty good."

That's the way she talked, the way she acted was much the same as Paul told me in the interview. I asked her: "Where did you come from...I mean, where did you grow up?"

She laughed, searched with her fingers between my legs and said: "A small cruddy dump of a town. The mayor did me when I was pretty young. My mother was dead and dad liked girls. Some people say he was a pig...that he didn't have any sense of morality. But it was at his suggestion that the mayor dicked me. So I got it."

Now to Paul's interview. He sat on the sofa, a cigarette in hand, and the mike in front of him.

"I'll tell you the kind of wife I have: When we were dating, she'd pull out my penis, play with it, saying all the time things like: 'I did this thing to Jimmy the other night. He liked it a lot. He wanted me to do this.' Then she leaned over and put her mouth on my joint. She always used to tell me about her other men. I found that it was sorta interesting. One story she told me was about the time she got three guys out in the country. They all stripped and then she lined them up side by side, and took them on, one at a time."

"Why did you marry her, Paul?"

"I sorta got to liking her. She's really a nice chick if you understand what I mean. She likes the same kind of things I like. She likes to have sexual relations at least twice a day—sometimes even four or five times. A guy can't keep up with her. I found that out right from the beginning."

"Then you love her?"

"I love her the most. I can't keep up with her, so I let her go out and have some guy. I then wait until she returns. Like the other night, she went out to a bar, after we had eaten dinner, and picked up this big muscle man. Afterwards, sometime about two in the morning, she returned, stripped naked, and then, as I began to get undressed, started to tell me what had happened.

"In the car she had placed her hand down between his legs, and played with his penis until it was hard as a rock, long and stiff like steel, squeezing, fondling, caressing. Then she unzipped him and touched his balls which were red hot in her fingers.

98

He laughed and then seemed to get a little excited, turned the car to the right, parked and then killed the engine.

"'Man, was he hung!' she said. 'I was so excited that I wanted to impale myself upon it right there. But the car wasn't the place. So I did him with my mouth. Oh, what a wonderful sensation it was.'

"At this point she laughed at me, her eyes looking at my penis which was as large as it could ever get. She stepped forward and mounted me. I must confess I didn't protest. What really surprised me was that with me inside her she continued with her story."

"You don't mind her telling you about her sexual adventures with other men?"

"Why should I?"

"You don't think it is unusual...a man letting his wife sleep out on him and...."

"Well, with this wife of mine...what can I do?"

"Ever wonder why you like it...? I mean, why you were willing to marry her?"

He thought about that for a moment, then said: "Not really. Other than the fact that she was the first girl I ever had. I came from a small town family, too. I knew little about sex. She is penis-happy and she seduced me on the first date. We were sitting in my old car and watching a movie—you know, the drive-ins—and she just reached out and groped me. I didn't know what to make of it, but she showed me the way to sexual pleasure. In other words, she performed fellatio—I think that's the technical term. That was my first introduction to sex."

"Did you like it?"

"Best of all what she did with her mouth. I liked

that best, because all I had to do was lay back and enjoy it. When you do the normal thing with a woman, you gotta worry about controlling yourself, about doing things right. It's some times hard to do right. Even with this wife of mine. So...I don't mind saying I like what she does with her lips on my penis."

"Does she like to have oral intercourse with you?"

"Yes. We both dig 69's."

"You ever do such things with a guy—or a guy do them to you?"

He gave me a furious look of anger, and then laughed, believing that I was joking. "You had me going there for a moment. Hell, I can't stand fags. The very idea is revolting...sickening. Those dirty, disgusting men. I don't know how they can do such things to one another."

"Like what?"

"Hell, you know, mutual masturbation, going down on one another...."

"Yet you like to do such things with your wife?"

"That's different. I'm a man and I like a woman. I love a woman. I like it all with a woman."

"Yet, how can you allow your wife to have other men?" Already I was beginning to guess his true problem, but was afraid to suggest it openly to him.

"Like I told you...no one man can keep her happy. She wants more than a guy can give. You know, once a day is pretty hard on a guy...that is, when you got a woman like her calling all the punches. She tells you all about the things she likes, tells you some real wild stories and then all the time she is playing with your dick and making you hard as hell and then when she puts it in her, you're all steamed up and you let loose, and everything drains out of you. She keeps at it until you can't take any more. Then she wants more and...hell, what do you do?"

"Don't you think it is unusual. I mean, the both of you?"

"Well, yes, I guess so."

"Have you thought of going to a marriage counselor and letting him help you out—I mean, find what makes your wife need sex so much."

"She's just sexy, wants it and I like her that way."

It was a stone-cold wall he'd put up and there wasn't any way to get around it. I knew from what little information I had, that if there ever was a latent homosexual, it was Paul. His interest in her telling about relations with other men was obviously a substitute for having homosexual experiences; his interest in a male's penis and his over-reaction towards homosexuals were all signs that Paul is emotionally becoming his wife as she has sex with other men; he sees himself in her role. Professional help would have been a smart move—possibly straightening Paul out either as a normal male or to acceptance of his homosexual desires. Either way he would have been far better off than with his wife, for she was a man eater. Her attitude towards him right from the beginning was dominating, uncaring and rather selfish.

What followed between me and his wife was somewhat unrestrained sex. I don't believe in recording my own experiences "for the record" since these case histories are about other people.

But I believe it would give a strong indication about the kind of wife Paul had, if I note what happened that evening when June had some to my apartment.

As I said, she had put her hand between my legs and it was impossible to ignore its touch.

"I like to feel a man's penis," June now announced, her fingers just boldly caressing me. "Why don't you just enjoy," she suggested, taking my right hand and putting it against her naked, warm crotch. "Finger me, if you want. And I'll give you head like you never experienced in all your life. I'm going to suck you off, like man, this is going to be simply great!"

She took me like Grant took Richmond.

COMMENT

I was some what uncomfortable at the thought of telling Paul what we had done. But it had been impossible to ignore her sexual advances. I knew that I would become a homosexual thrill for Paul.

But the fact remains that a woman is the seducer, since they are the ones who must uncross their legs; in June's case, her legs were wide open from the moment she stepped into the room and she went after what she wanted in a direct and forward manner which left no room for refusal. Her desperation, her actions and attitudes had been almost frantic. When she took me into her mouth, she went crazy, like a mad-woman, yet it seemed as if she were almost too excited, as if attempting to convince herself that it was a lot of fun. She seemed, in some ways even detached, in the manner she gave instructions, the manner she demanded me to pinch her nipples, the automatic way in which she went from one move to the next. My guess is that she, too, has a leaning toward homosexuality —or is actually frigid; a common trait for a woman who acts in her manner.

There was little to say to Paul, since he didn't seem to know really what was wrong with him. The fact is that he did feel some compulsion to tell somebody else about his sexual experiences. I couldn't really convince him that professional help might be best, and he left much the same as he came, little changed for his experience in so-called confession. After his wife had left that evening, I understood a little more about the kind of woman she was, and therefore the kind of strange marriage he had. They were suited to one another, living a kind of private hell that most people would never be able to be happy in. Possibly they were as happy as they could ever be.

Sometimes it is best not to fix something which is working. And for them, their relationship seemed to be a solution to their needs.

Perhaps, in the long run, the lesson to be learned from their shared experiences is that people generally find a partner who fits their needs. They certainly seemed will suited to one another.

CHAPTER SEVEN

Karen's Hunger for Older Men

Karen, a blonde girl in her early twenties, dated me a couple of times and then we became more or less friends once I learned the kind of woman she was. Karen liked older men, and that was it. She would tease and even have sexual intercourse with a man her own age, but didn't really enjoy it unless a lot of teasing was involved. With an older man, it was different. In time she willingly allowed me to tape the story of her experiences. "I was eighteen when I got laid the first time," Karen announced, taking a deep drag on her cigarette. "The way it happened...well, it might be of some interest to you. I was staying with my uncle, he's married to my aunt, my mother's sister. He was also carrying on an affair with a younger woman—not much older than myself. I was dating his son from another marriage, a young man about twenty-five, at the time. I'll call him John.

"After going to a movie, we came home early to discover the place empty. John got out a bottle of whiskey, asked if I wanted a drink. I'd had only a few drinks in the past, in secret with dates. The idea appealed to me. John is a handsome bull—and I was turned on by his good looks. He played football in school and I was pretty sure he had the kind of muscular build that would make any woman get hot by just looking at him. I hadn't seen him in a bathing suit, but wanted to.

"We had a drink in the living room. He turned down the lights, put the radio on, romantic music and then sat down beside me on the sofa. He placed an arm about my shoulders as we sipped our drinks. The mood was intimate and inviting and when he turned to kiss me, I was more than willing to play the necking game. What I didn't know was that John wanted more than mere necking—and I wanted the same thing, but would not have admitted it to myself. The drink had made me a little flushed and when he frenched me, I got a little excited. Then I felt his right hand reach under my sweater and up toward my breast. The tingling sensation that ripped through me was just too much. I thought it wouldn't do any harm to let him touch my breasts. We could always put up the stop signs. When his hand covered my crotch I sorta went wild, straining up against his large hand, which quickly caressed downward, thrillingly. I was already swelled up and hurting. Then suddenly his hand was under my skirt, up and above the nylon stockings, caressing my naked thighs. Then it slipped under my panties. When he ran his finger into my vagina I couldn't stand it. No guy had ever done anything like that to me before. His other hand was pulling up my sweater, above the bra. A moment later he had unlatched the bra and before I knew it I felt his lips close about one nipple. Soon he went all the way with me.

"He was making love to me for the third time when the lights went on and Uncle Ben was standing in the entrance of the living room. My aunt was out of town that week-end and he had just come home from a date with his mistress. He took one look at what was happening and then screamed at John at the top of his lungs. John leaped up and quickly ran out of the room. Uncle Ben, a large, powerful man, slammed across the floor towards the sofa, slapped out a large hand, which struck my face so hard that I was numbed. Then all at once I was lying over his lap and his hand was hitting my fanny again and again and again, stinging, hurting, but suddenly so thrilling that I sobbed, crying out, hitting the sofa with clutched fists. I must have had half a dozen orgasms before he realized what was happening and stopped. Disgusted, he left the room.

"I was pretty shocked at what had happened, ashamed like you don't know how. John had left me high and Uncle Ben had beaten me to orgasm. It was quite an education on sex, all at once. I ran up to the room I was staying in and cried all night."

I asked what happened after that.

"Uncle Ben sent John away and then told me that I had to leave, but would have to see a doctor the next morning before returning home. We agreed that it would be best to keep the whole thing quiet from my parents."

"Then they never found out?"

"No. It would have blown the whole family sky high. The folks had never told me much about sex and so...they were a little stiff about it."

"When did you have sex again?"

"Just about three months later. I was turned on by then. I was sure about how to take care of myself, because the doctor Uncle Ben had taken me to had told me much about such matters. I was out on a date with a young man and we ended up at a drive-in movie and I suddenly wanted sex but bad. I let him play with me and I reciprocated. But I never let him get into me. He nearly blew his mind from frustration. I, however, found teasing him so wild that I came—not once but several times."

"Why didn't you let him have sexual intercourse with you?"

"It was more fun that way. I have learned a lot about myself since then. I like a cock—but I have to get it my own way. Another guy, some months later, really got to me. He was about twenty-nine, been in the service and probably had enough girls to know the score. We went to his apartment, had drinks and then at his suggestion we got undressed. When I hesitated at his suggestion, he said:

"'Look, baby, I don't have the time to play around...get undressed or I'll beat the hell out of you.' When I hesitated again, he grabbed me and almost tore my blouse off. I got the idea, and fast. The roughness was different—just...wild. I was soon naked and then he started to fondle one of my breasts. I squeezed hard on him and suddenly wanted desperately to hurt him, so I twisted on that stick in my hand. He let out a yell, squeezed hard on my breast and then slapped my face a stunning blow. I fell back, stumbling over a foot stool and landed on the sofa, legs spread, dangling. He leaped at me and suddenly slapped my face again, a stunning blow. The next thing I knew was he'd put the long shaft deep into me.

"Almost immediately I achieved orgasm, and as he kept ramming himself against me, faster and faster, I experienced several orgasms. It was far greater than I'd ever known it to be."

"But you said that there weren't really any sexual experiences—before this—I mean, normal, regular experiences to compare—"

"It was my first real understanding of the pleasure of pain. I connected it with the multiple orgasms. But I hadn't learned all there was to know about my need to be hit—to be hurt—in connection with sex."

"When did you learn the full extent of your need for pain during sexual intercourse?"

"With an older man, well in his forties. I was working as his secretary and he took me to a motel one night and we stripped. He reached for me and I wanted to tease him like I'd done with other guys more my age. But I learned a total lesson that night. I guess you want me to tell you about that."

"If you wish to."

"Why not? He was strong, but a little heavy. When I reached down and grabbed his limp stick and pulled on it real hard, actually attempting to hurt him, he got very mad. I don't know what made me do it. I wanted sex with him for several reasons. I believe one reason was the fact that he was married and I liked the idea of having a married man—or proving that a married man could desire me—that I was something better than his wife. I wanted to feel the hardness of him, but it was limp in my hands, and I pulled on it and I got suddenly frightened that it wouldn't get hard and that he couldn't satisfy me. And then, I don't know...maybe I wanted to be hit—I guess that was part of it. I wanted to be hit hard, and he was the kind of guy who hit-—and so hard that I couldn't believe it. His fists slammed at my face and I fell on the bed, half conscious. What I didn't know was that he wanted to hurt women, too. So we fit, in that way. He came at me like a savage, his teeth ground on my breasts. He slapped my face again and again in a fury of rage and I felt him getting damned hard between my legs. I started doing things to him with my nails, slashing at his back, hard. The harder I slashed the harder he got and the more he hit me...I was getting orgasms before he even put that long stick into me."

She laughed in delight. "That was real good and afterwards we both laughed and I suggested he spank me—or was it his suggestion? I don't know—but the thing is he spanked me, pulling my hips over his legs and hit my fanny again and again until I screamed out in painful joy. It felt so damned good, so wonderful—hell, I had one orgasm after another. We continued our affair for a long time and it was just so wild. It's been like that with every older man I've had since. I tease and taunt them and drive them to the point where they spank me real hard and then we do the whole bit. With men my own age I just have...well, I'll let them have me after I've teased the hell out of them. It's the only way I can enjoy sexual relations—otherwise it's dullsville."

COMMENT

Even though Karen didn't seem to feel great guilts about her sexual habits, she did, upon my suggestion, consult a professional therapist and was quite interested in doing so, since she realized that her sexual habits were not considered the standard "norm"—but what happened to her after that I really don't know. The therapist who saw her half a dozen times said he had lost contact with her and that she did seem to have a greater understanding of what made her tick.

Though he wasn't willing to talk about her case in any details, he did admit to me that: "She seems to be okay. What that might mean, I can't say. My experience has been that curing isn't the issue, but rather gaining greater understanding of how to deal with these feelings and needs in their lives. Regardless of what they end up doing, if they grow, that's all that counts."

It was obvious that Karen had equated young men as being unable to fully satisfy her—and the spanking her uncle had given her had created a sharp guilt concerning sexual relations with men, plus the complication of having achieved sexual satisfaction by the spanking. She was frightened by sex, felt great guilts and had to be punished for feeling excited before really achieving orgasm. There are a lot of men and women much like Karen in one extent or another, and once they learn how to understand their drives, and forget their guilts about sex, and learn to know that the sexual side of life is a normal function of the human body and emotions and not something animal and disgusting or something to feel guilty about, they manage to find a normal adjustment in life and gain a normal, happy relationship with a husband or wife and live contented lives, which allow total enjoyment of sexual relations with somebody they love and who loves them.

Many continue practicing these methods towards a satisfactory life (to them), wanting to enjoy a more aggressive sexual experience. Some lighten up and play-act such sexual practices, allowing some minor pain, under their control, with special code words that say "back off, honey!"

It is all a matter of taste, and limits and what makes a person happy. If that's what turns on an otherwise fairly normal person, as long as it doesn't hurt anybody else, that's one thing; if, on the other hand a person is unhappy, feels guilts and torments concerning such needs and hungers, the solution is getting professional help to gain greater understanding as to what motivates them. Even if that's not a total so-called "cure" it does offer a road to greater happiness.

Much like the with the gay person, there isn't a cure, but there are solutions which allow for greater understanding of what they are all about and how to deal that into their lives in such a way that make enhances rather than cripples them. Self acceptance and understanding can do wonders. And what is "normal" for one person may not be the same for another. Each of us has to discover our own limits and our own way to achieve a satisfactory love life.

People like Karen need to understand what makes them run like they do, and once that happens they had a richer, more rewarding living experience.

CHAPTER EIGHT

The Call Girl: Norma

Norma is a prostitute, highly attractive, blonde haired, classic face, with a lovely body that moves gracefully. She came to me quite by accident, through a bartender friend, who introduced us. She was more than willing to tell her story, feeling that it might help other girls to understand the position of the prostitute and teach them the pitfalls that follow this profession.

"I'm what one might call," she told me in her apartment, "a lesbian—because I found out early in life that it was impossible to enjoy a man in a sexual way—not after having become a professional prostitute. In the beginning, young enough not to know what sex was all about, I enjoyed men—but that was nothing more than a normal interest in sexual thrills—which men cannot give me. But the first time was just fine."

"Do you want to go into details about it?"

"You mean about my first experiences?"

"If you think they are meaningful," I suggested in a casual manner.

"To me they were meaningful—and I guess it would set the tone, give you a true picture of what being a prostitute can do to a girl."

"Can you remember much about the first man you ever had?"

"I can remember just about everything—as if it were last night. A lot of men have gone through my life since then, but the first was the most impressive. My family had taken me up to the mountains for our summer vacation. The place was beautiful, snow capped peaks, fleecy clouds, clear sky. It was a little cold, but one could get their hands over a roaring fire and warm up pretty quick. This place was one of those out of the way spots, where everybody ate together, sang and danced in the evenings—and got to know each other.

"I was old enough to be allowed a drink, from my parents' point of view. There weren't more than half a dozen couples there with their children. It was like one happy family, in more than one way, I learned. Before the two weeks were up, some wife swapping had taken place. I made friends with a girl—I guess she was just about one year younger than myself. Call her Connie. She was beautiful, well developed and knew her way around men. I was surprised by that, because I'd never been had. In a way I thought of her as being a little fast. Funny, when you come to think of it, because she is married and has three children, from the last report.

"She came on fast with men—I took longer to start; she got herself pregnant—I learned the ropes fast and developed a keen interest in sex as kicks, kicks and a way to make money, because I happened to fall in with the right crowd.

"We were walking along the tree-lined brook that ran behind the main lodge where everybody gathered until the late hours, when they would disappear for a short time and then return to their own cabins.

"It was early and the sun had just set. We sat down on some rocks, watching the water and suddenly Connie asked: 'Ever have a guy before?' I shook my head and she looked at me as if I was out of my mind, 'Why? Don't you like the idea?' I considered this for a moment, then said: "I never considered it. Why did you ask?" She laughed, said: 'Well, considering you're old enough to be living on your own...well, in any case, this is the place to get a man.' We talked generally, then she said: 'Carl screwed me last night. He has the biggest cock I've ever had. I went crazy. He had me go down on him, never done anything like that before. It was treats from the beginning. If you want to get laid, he's the guy for you.'

"She went on like that for some time, but I finally said: 'But Carl's married.' She laughed at me. 'He's on the make for anything with skirts on. His wife...she knows, but doesn't seem to mind. I haven't seen her letting the other men play bed-games with her, but she doesn't seem to mind.' I asked Connie about her sex life and she said: 'When I was much younger, I used to tease my older brother. We would get on the bed, naked and I'd jerk him off. It was fun. That's how I learned about a man. We never did anything more than that together—after all, we were brother and sister. One of his boy friends, at a make-out party, got me in a bedroom and made me masturbate him, like I'd done with my

114

brother, but he wanted to take my cherry too, and I let him. Didn't even hurt, really. Maybe it was… broken…before. I don't know. Just know it was great! What a ball that was.'

"I was shocked by her conversation and bold talk about sex, but also interested to the point where I determined to get to Carl that evening. It galled me to think that this girl, who was younger than myself, was so experienced and I'd never had a man before. The whole idea seemed right. So, after dinner, when the wine was being poured, I managed to go up to Carl, who was standing with his wife, and begin a casual conversation. He was immediately attentive to me. It was obvious that he considered my friend-liness as an open pass and he played right along with it. Some time later, when my wine glass was empty, he asked if I'd like another drink, and I said, yes. He took my arm, squeezing it lightly with strong fingers and told me to come with him. We walked into the kitchen, which was open to the guests at the lodge—the place was like family in that way—and he looked on the shelves for a bottle. He cursed, said: 'Golly be, I left it back at the cabin.' I took the hint and suggested that we might go there and get it. It was what he was waiting for. As we stepped out into the cool night air, Carl looked at me, said: 'You certainly are a beautiful young woman. I've never seen such a classic and lovely face...and I must say that you have matured wonderfully.' His eyes swept down my figure and there was no question about what he was talking about; or what he wanted.

"We walked arm in arm to his cabin and when the door had been closed behind us, he quickly went to the small kitchen—the cabins were three to four roomed—and came back with whiskey and two glasses. 'Want to drink it here or go back to the party?' he asked, standing directly in front of me, staring into my eyes. 'It's sorta fun doing it here,' I stated in such a manner that he would know exactly what I meant.

"So we sat on the soft sofa and he poured the drinks, handed me one. I was flushed with excitement and felt quite bold. After having part of the whiskey, I told him: "Connie said you were real nice to her last night.' He seemed surprised by that, but grinned, saying, 'She was a nice young lady. She was very nice to me. I enjoyed her company very much.' I laughed, asked: 'Is that all you enjoyed?' That made him laugh, too, and then he placed an arm about my shoulder, drawing me close. His voice was husky as he told me, 'A girl like Connie is nothing next to you. I'm only surprised that she said anything about last night.' I shrugged, looked up into his eyes and explained: 'She told me just about everything that went on between the two of you—about the offer of a drink and you not finding it in the kitchen and then bringing her here and how you played coy for some time and then seduced her. She could hardly wait until you got undressed.'

"I felt bold and slightly high and had made my decision to go through with this thing. He gazed seriously at me and asked: 'How do you feel about that?' I played coy with: 'About what?" He put his hand down on my right thigh, caressed it and asked: 'About me getting naked?' I boldly came right out and said: 'Isn't that what both of us are here for?'

He chuckled, stood arid went to the front door, latched it and turned to face me. 'I didn't think you were that kind of girl,' he stated, giving my body such a burning lustful look that I already felt naked. 'What kind of girl did you think I was?' I countered, standing, wanting to appear experienced. He merely shrugged, his eyes level with mine. Then he said:

"'Why don't you *tell* me what kind of girl you are?' I merely took off my sweater, and felt excited by this act. He feasted upon my bra-covered breasts. I had large, well-developed breasts even then. 'I'm a girl who wants a man to make love to me,' I told him boldly, reaching around and unlatching my bra. 'Why don't you make love to me?' His eyes seemed to pop out of their sockets as my breasts fell free from the bra.

"He took one long look and then came at me like a charging bull, falling on his knees. His mouth on my breasts, his hands slipped under my skirt. The next second my panties were off and he started exploring my vagina with an expert care. Then he pulled my skirt up over my waist and started spearing me with his tongue. It was driving me out of my mind, sending shivers of pleasure through my body so wildly that I couldn't stand it. Finally he stood, looked down at me and said: 'Let's...get undressed, together,' I was so ready that I couldn't move and he had to help me undress. It was good, the way he undressed me. I came I don't know how many times. Afterwards I just fell back on the bed, unconscious."

"Did you do it again with him?"

"No. That was the end of the show. I don't think he could've done it again, anyway. He'd done wonderfully, that time."

"You seemed to like it with him, what happened the next time you were seduced—what made it different?"

"Several things. One was that the guy was a bastard; a dirty foul-assed bastard, I was in college and was working at a restaurant—one of those small places which serve the college students—working my way through, because I wanted to be totally on my own. This guy, Billy, he ran the place. He was a burly man, with a beard and a large stomach and a pair of beady eyes. From the first day he had kept his eyes on me. Then one night, when we closed late, he offered me a drink. He lived in the back, a small room. Here we sat on a dirty sofa, and he poured me a stiff drink. After we'd had one drink and I was about to leave, he offered another drink. His eyes were always looking at my figure with such open lust that I couldn't help knowing what he had in mind."

"How'd it happen?"

"I'm getting to it, don't be greedy," she said with a grim smile. "Suddenly he said, after the second drink, 'I think you're cute. And I want to lay you.' Just like that. I got up and started to leave, but he grabbed hold of my arm, said:

"'Look, baby, you treat me right and I'll see to it you get along just fine here at the college.' I demanded what he meant by that. 'Just that you treat me right, or I'll say you've been laying the guys here for money.' I stared at him, unable to believe his words. 'What the hell do you mean?' I cried, hands on hips. 'I mean that a lot of the girls who work here are putting out—I got into some trouble about this one time, and if I turned you in and the other girls supported my story, you'd be in jail—you'd be in hot trouble. Just treat me right and everything will be okay.'

"I was just young enough to believe his con, 'I'll give you a raise—you just have to give me a little.' He was glaring at my breasts and it was obvious what he wanted to do. I started to turn, in order to leave immediately, but he grabbed hold of my shoulder, spun me around and said:

"'Baby, you're going to get it, one way or another—so why don't you just play along with the game. Either you get it or I'll fix you up real good.' Can you believe it? He was threatening me, and I was scared silly. I started to say something, but he suddenly hit me real hard, 'You get undressed, girl; or you'll be undressed and I won't be gentle about it!'

"I was scared and did exactly as he said. Then he pulled down his pants, exposing himself, I was amazed by his largeness. He told me to get down on my hands and knees and do him. 'You do that baby, you just do that, or else.' I started to hesitate and he slapped me again and again, from one side of the face to the other. Then his big strong hands grabbed my shoulders and forced me to my knees, I thought of screaming, but realized that the place was deserted. His coffee shop was miles from the college and in an area where little traffic passed at this time of night, Suddenly I realized that I was totally helpless. There wasn't anything I could do, so I leaned forward and did as he commanded.

"After he came he opened the back door of his small room and said: 'Okay, boys, come on in, she's ready for you.' I was convulsed on the floor and when I looked up there were two young college men, naked. One grabbed me from behind and flung me to the bed on my back as the other yanked my legs apart. They both stuck me time and time again, while I sobbed and screamed and pleaded. I felt some pleasure. Once they were finished I screamed I was going to the police. They merely laughed, my boss saying that all would swear I had offered myself for money. He finished with, 'I have several girl friends around who will also state that you had talked to them about setting yourself up as a prostitute. If I were you, I'd just let it lay there. We've made a collection for you—twenty-five dollars. That should pay for your trouble.' With that they shoved the money into my hand and said I'd better get dressed and leave. I not only left, but I also left the town, finding a job in a restaurant some fifty miles away and taking an apartment with one of the other girls. It turned out that this room-mate of mine was bi-sexual and enjoyed it with both men and girls in quite a fashion. Once she had a couple of boys up and we did a circus thing, you know what that is?"

"What kind of circus?"

"Well, this kind of thing, like one boy would go down on me and I'd go down on another guy, who was in turn going down on my roommate who did it to the guy kissing me off. I learned quite a lot of tricks during this period, one being to play for pay. She would get plenty of gifts for sessions with men and we got to talking one day and decided there wasn't any reason we couldn't pick up some cash for doing what we were doing for free."

"How'd you feel about all this? Didn't you feel cheap?"

"Not in the least. You have to remember that I had been raped by the guy Bill and his two friends. Nothing after that made me feel cheap. After as many years as I've been at it a girl gets totally cold to men in a sexual way."

"Haven't you ever wanted children?"

"I almost had a couple...but was lucky to find a friendly doctor. No, I don't want children. I like my life. In a few years I'll be able to retire and then a girl I know will come and live with me in some nice house I'll buy and we'll live happily forever after." Her voice hesitated, sounded thoughtful for a moment, then she added: "But I'll admit, sometimes I wish I had married some nice guy and never learned about the sordid side of life, That's the price I have to pay for being in the profession I've been in all my life. But you can't have everything. Men don't want whores as wives and that's it."

"You've never had a satisfactory relationship with a man outside of the very first time?" I asked, a little puzzled by her.

"There was one, but he's totally off the record, He was married and of great political importance. He's the only one, but he died not too long ago and...well, I'd just as soon forget it. It was an accident and it won't happen again, for there will never be another like him." She shrugged and then said: 'I think that just about lines it up, doesn't it,"

"Anything else?"

"No. Only that I'd never suggest prostitution to a girl who wants a family or a true lover. I'd change things, myself, if it were possible—I guess. No, maybe I wouldn't. Some girls are just whores—I guess that's my life's story. Everything else is just repetition of what has happened to me in those first youthful experiences that led me into my profession."

She hesitated, then added: "That's my story. But every call-girl or street whore and the likes all have different stories. Some girls come from homes where they were sexually abused and are trying to make it on the streets, and have no other way. Some are kind of seduced by pimps or even forced into it. Life can be tough on the streets of a big city for a young girl without any working experience and desperate. Some are loose, bluntly put. They want sex for any of a number of reasons and decide to make some fast bucks doing it. Some just have private reasons. All...pay a heavy price. Some do get married, usually without revealing their past life. And some shack up with a guy who knows their past life—again, we're all different. But what I've told you is my story."

She had closed the topic and didn't want to talk about it further. She offered to let me have sex with her for a cut-rate, but I thanked her and said I had some important business for that evening. She walked out, saying: "Any time you want a service job, I'll give you one for half price."

I thanked her and then she left.

COMMENT

There seemed something sad about Norma. Her hatred for men no doubt went deeper than mere sexual exhaustion—her attitude about life and her place in the world, seemed depressive. I couldn't help but think if she could wave a magic wand and erase all that had happened to her, and find a normal relationship with a man she loved, Norma would have done so. But she had convinced herself that she was happy—as far as it went. Her warning to other girls, who might seek out the same kind of profession, seemed to suggest her own inner longing but she just barely admitted to that.

I wonder if Norma will ever find happiness, if she will ever discover there is a place for a woman like her, other than in some cheap hotel room with a play for pay guy. She, like so many people, simply passed out of my life. I assume she continued her profession; I would assume she will end up in some home, paid for by prostituting her body, living with other women.

There are so many girls like Norma, who get into prostitution because they decide that getting paid for it is better than giving it out for free. Street prostitutes or escort services, the call-girl racket, call it what you want, but this is a harder, more dangerous and difficult solution to surviving. Broken homes, abuse or just teenage rebellion can be the shove which starts them on this kind of pathway. A sad reality. How much better to some how bite the bullet, get an education, a job and work one's way up through the system, rather than ending up on the streets selling their bodies. Most end up drugged, hooked for life, or with AIDS. A few even go into hard core pornography to make fast bucks. Once down this dead-end trail it becomes even more difficult to escape the horrors, to turn their lives around and find happiness.

Sure, a girl can put out for money—but that's all she will get out of the relationship. Few men fall for this kind of woman, and they don't fool themselves into believing it is a romantic interlude. How sad to be nothing but a depository for a man's released tensions—and not a thing to be loved.

CHAPTER NINE

Virgin/Whore—Hank

Here the "Summary" comes first, insofar as indicating that what follows is a prime example of the male who considers women Virgins or Whores and doesn't realize there is a vast middle ground which has nothing to do with either extreme. This is an example of a false concept concerning women. It can lead to all kinds of distortions later in life—even in a good, otherwise, healthy marriage.

Though this conversational exchange took place some time ago, and the Aids problems of the last decades has changed some of the social habits of dating, where Condoms are a required part of safe sex, what is said here still applies: women aren't just Goddess Virgins or Cheap Tramps! Those that *do* and those that *don't*! And the sexual side of life is far more complex than such a simpleminded approach might suggest. Yet many men grow up believing as Hank did—and thus limit their options. Most importantly, they miss out on a real relationship with a wonderful woman. Well, now to let Hank speak for himself, and allow my comments to remain within the context of our taped conversation:

* * * * * * *

"There are two kinds of girls," Hank told me in a very serious, convincing manner, over a martini cocktail: "The ones that will and the ones that won't."

"A very interesting observation on your part," I countered, trying to keep my face straight. I'd met Hank at a cocktail lounge in Hollywood. We hadn't seen each other for some years and it was old home week. Hank is a highly successful insurance sales-man who keeps on the move and makes a lot of money. We'd been drinking and talking for some time, and the martinis were beginning to have their effects on us. "How do you tell the difference?"

He grinned and swallowed down the rest of his drink, "You can't tell from looking at them, but you can tell after you have considered where you met them. Now take that girl down at the end of the bar. She's the kind that will, I'll bet you anything."

"How much do you want to put on the line," I inquired.

"Five dollars?" he suggested, grinning.

"Five dollars!"

"I'll see you later—I do have your address, don't I?"

"Yes," I assured him as he moved off the bar-stool.

"Well, see you later, buddy," he announced again, showing little effects from the martinis. He made his way to the attractive blonde who was dressed in a nicely fitting cocktail dress. I watched as he approached her and after a few words sat down next to her. I ordered another cocktail and waited, interested in what would happen next, I hadn't finished the drink when the two suddenly stood and walked out of the cocktail lounge to-gether. After finishing the drink I left and returned to my apartment, watched television and then went to bed about twelve-thirty. It seemed as if I'd just fallen to sleep, though three hours had passed, when the front door bell rang. Dazed, irritated at being awakened in the middle of the night, I pulled on a bathrobe and went to the front door, opening it.

There stood Hank, a wide grin on his face.

"What the hell are you doing here?" I cried, stepping back in alarm.

"To collect five dollars, buddy," he grinned, moving into the room. "I told you I would be seeing you later."

I shook my head and closed the door, turned and faced him. "Do you know what time it is?"

"Sure do, buddy, about three-thirty. We had a swinging time. What a chick, tits like you can't imagine, grinding hips and voluptuous lips. We went to a motel and swung like crazy. She turned on immediately. I told you there are girls that do and girls that don't."

Awake and resigned, because I knew that Hank was turned on and wanted to talk, I asked: "Want some coffee?"

"Anything stronger, buddy?" he inquired, sitting down on the sofa.

"Whiskey."

"Fine."

"Okay, I'll join you," I announced, knowing it

was going to be a long stand.

As I fixed the drinks, Hank spotted a shelf of my own books in the living room.

"You write these?" he asked. "You weren't kidding, were you?"

"I'm a professional working writer and I write what the public wants—which means: what the publishers want and pay hard cold cash for."

"Man, man, that's pretty wild stuff." I returned to the living room with two strong whiskies and sat down on the sofa. We talked about my writing and I mentioned the book I was in the process of producing at the time.

"That's pretty wild stuff," he commented, after thumbing through one of the books he had picked out of shelf. "Where do you get your information?"

"Various places. But in the factual 'case history' books I have to rely on people telling their stories."

"Oh, what kind of material?" he inquired, grinning.

I pulled out a chapter of the book I was working on and he quickly glanced through it, impressed by its honesty.

"People don't pull any punches, do they?" he asked, looking up at me in a serious manner. "You don't...well, just make it up, do you?"

"Look, friend, stuff like this you don't make up—I have tapes to back roost of it in detail...some of the tapes I've had to erase because well, one could end up with a whole house full of useless tapes. People are funny—they get to talking to me as if...well, they don't seem to mind just bluntly giving out with frank, detailed remarks."

"This stuff is true?"

"At least true insofar as a correct transcript of what they told me."

He nodded, then sipped his drink. "Then what went on tonight would interest you plenty."

I considered and mentally rejected his offer, but could see it would hurt him if I didn't bite to the bait.

"Why don't you tell me about it," I suggested, feeling trapped.

"Hell, buddy, I'll just do that."

He waited and I waited.

"Well, don't you want to get your tape recorder?" Hank inquired.

Suddenly I realized what he was expecting and felt a sinking sensation. Obviously Hank had misunderstood the purpose of my book and believed that a pure sexual experience was all I wanted. But I couldn't hurt a friend, so I set up the tape recorder and then placed the mike in front of him.

"Well, go on," I suggested.

"Just like that?" He seemed ill-at-ease, puzzled.

"Just like that."

"Where do I begin?"

"Well, you bet me five dollars that she was the kind of woman who would—you went over and had a conversation with her and then the two of you left, went to a motel room and—"

"You want me to tell you about what happened in the motel room?" he asked, as if the whole idea was startling.

"Isn't that what you wanted to tell me?"

He nodded and said: "Yes, I guess so. I guess so." He was thoughtful for a moment, then said:

"You know, Carson, I've had a funny kind of

sex life."

Immediately my ears picked up. "In what way?"

"Well...how would one put it...maybe from the beginning...maybe that would be the best way."

"Where is the beginning?"

"In college, I guess. Believe it or not I was a virgin when I entered college. I didn't know anything about girls. Then one of the guys says he knows a doll that will put out—that she'll take on all the guys who want to ball her. To be truthful it was one disgusting event. But it was my introduction to sex. I was turned on and wanted to find me a nice girl to have an affair with."

"Did you find such a girl?"

"I was told about another young girl who put out to the guys, asked her for a date, which she accepted. We went out into the country with blanket and lunch. She lay on her back, looking up at me in a very wanton fashion. I just watched her, wanting like hell to reach out and kiss her lips, but afraid to make the first move. We talked for some time, then she asked: 'Would you like to make love to me?' I managed to say something, but can't remember what. She pulled up her white blouse and then sitting up, removed her bra. Exposing her breasts, she said: 'Kiss them, I like them to be kissed.' Naturally I complied. She, in turn, started to play around with my cock. She was really an aggressive chick. Before I knew it she had pulled my pants down and was really having a field day. She seemed to be nympho. We both seemed to go off right together. It was a wild afternoon, I'll tell you."

"Did you see her again?"

"Several times during the college year."

"What did you think of her?"

"What do you mean?"

"Well, did you like her a lot?"

"Hell, yes. She was really good."

"Love her?"

"The ones I fall in love with?"

"That was what I had in mind. I'm very interested in the difference."

"I treat them with respect."

"Have they ever made passes?"

"No. A nice girl doesn't go for such things."

"You know, Hank, I met a girl once who was very nice. She never came out and said she wanted to go to bed with me. We dated. We talked about sex, but she was shy about it. Then one day, we were listening to records in my apartment, and I had served a couple of drinks. We got to kissing, and then suddenly I got a little excited and started to caress her breasts. She struggled slightly, but then suddenly went wild. She helped me get undressed, and to my amazement, she became aggressive. She sat before me, her large breasts thrusting, then she lowered my head between her legs and lay back, sobbing from joy.

"When I entered her, I thought she might be a virgin, but discovered she wasn't. Afterwards, we got to talking and she said that she'd had quite a few men, but was afraid to make any aggressive move until the man made the first one, that she didn't want any guy to think she was cheap, that she simply liked sex like a man, but wanted romance mixed with it. She said that too many men had the idea that nice girls wouldn't and those that would were not nice girls. It was my first real experience with a woman who gave every indication of never allowing a man to touch her, but was quickly willing to tell a lot about her sexual experiences and admit that it was difficult to appear respectable and have affairs. Her attitude was that sex was a healthy part of life, and that it was all right to have a lover—have an affair, love affair if you will—but thought it was too cheap and dirty to just allow herself to be picked up by any stud on the make. And when I tell you she was respectable, I mean just that. Most women over twenty-one who are worth beans, have been had, simply because they want to give themselves. And if you believe it or not, the act of sexual intercourse to a nice girl is an act of giving herself to the man she loves. She wants to give him pleasure, she wants to feel the joy of having shared something beautiful with him. She doesn't even need an orgasm.

"This particular girl told me that, too, which I've found to be supported by many medical authorities. A woman is human and she has sexual desires and wants to give herself to her lover. If a man doesn't take the aggressive stand, or at least indicate that he desires her, she gets frustrated. She wants him, she wonders why he doesn't want her. She considers his lack of advances as being a lack of interest, an insult, a turning down, or far worse believes there might be something wrong with him. Consider for a moment, was there any time, when you were with a girl you had fallen in love with, that she gave any indication that she might want to go to bed with you? Was there any time when you were puzzled, mystified, unsure of a so-called 'nice' girl opposed to a so-called 'play-girl'?"

Hank thought that one over and then looked up

at me in amazement. "Come to think of it, the last girl I was seriously dating, once invited me up for cocktails, after we'd seen a movie. She put on music, turned down the lights, lighted a candle and, believe me, if she'd been some girl I'd picked up, it would have been obvious what she wanted. She snuggled close to me, put my arm around her shoulders. I didn't roll with the punches, because...well, she was a girl I loved and I wouldn't insult her by trying to seduce her. Seduction in my mind is nothing much more than rape. You're forcing the girl to do something against her will—you are overwhelming her body, making her unable to control the basic animal instincts. It would be a dirty trick! But come to think of it...why that young witch. I bet you're right!"

"Not the way you seem to think. Ever consider that a woman can not be seduced if she keeps her legs crossed. She's the one who has to say yes. She's the one who puts up the stop signals—not the man. And if the man doesn't even try, if he's the one who is putting up the stop signals, hell, what do you think a healthy young woman thinks? Either there is something wrong with her or there is something wrong with him. What do you think she is going to believe?"

"Damn it, Carson, you make every woman sound like a slutting tramp."

"No I don't."

"Hell you don't. You just said that every woman wants to be laid. Aren't there any nice girls left in the world? Are they all whores?"

"No—and I don't even think the ones who are easy pick-ups are whores, either. Being single can

133

be a very lonely life —and a woman, just like a man, wants companionship, she wants to be loved, and she wants a man to desire her. Some women are more sexually hungry than others, some are desperately trying to prove to themselves that they really like sex—some are just desperate that they will never get a man—there are as many reasons for a girl putting out to a man as there are women. But this term, 'putting out' is a little crude. I like a more sane expression: giving themselves totally to a partner—usually of the opposite sex. They are mature, adult, and have physical and sexual and emotional hungers which can only be satisfied through love affairs. You're a damned fool. You've probably been turning off some of the best romances you could ever have.

"And," I added seriously, "did you ever consider the idea that all women are different, that there are actually some girls who might be a good sexual partner for you—for life? You marry a girl without having had an affair with her, and you might just discover that you aren't matched sexually. I learned a long time ago that the first thing a man should get out of the way is the sexual side of a relationship. Hell, how do you know if it's just sex that you're after when you 'fall in love' with a 'nice' girl? How do you know that she is right for you in every way? Not that it is required or expected, but in too many cases it is smart to discover as much as possible before binding a relationship into a legal tangle. Marriage is too difficult without complicating it unnecessarily right at the start.

"If you want to marry a girl without having experienced the total sharing of one another, without knowing all there is to know about one another without having lived for several years together, that's up to you—you'll find a girl who finally says yes to your offer of marriage, and it might work out just fine—many such marriages are successful. But marriage is a long-term investment, and there are enough problems to face and solve, without adding to them by discovering that there is no real sexual unity between you. And what could be far more terrible is to discover after the wedding night that the only thing you were really in love with was getting into her pants. You can't survive in a marriage where there is only sexual interest, easily satisfied by a jump in bed—there has to be more to it than that."

I took a swallow of my whiskey and realized that I hadn't given him the total picture. "Hank, what I'm trying to say is that the way you're going, you'll never find the right kind of woman. The kind of woman you're looking for exists in fantasy, in romantic novels—and generally does not happen in life. You will probably end up marrying some nice girl you thought was a virgin, only to discover, too late, that she was just a normal healthy woman. I'm not saying that kids should experiment with sex—that's something totally different. A kid doesn't know what ends up. They couldn't take on the responsibility if the girl got pregnant, and chances are the girl they think they desire as a young kid is not the person they want as a mature adult. But, hell, man, you're old enough to know better. I'm surprised at you."

He looked up at me, grinning. "I'm full of surprises, aren't I?"

I laughed. "Guess you are. I thought you were a man of the world and now I find you are a romantic fool. Nothing wrong with that, really, but blast it all, Hank, you should face up to the fact that there aren't really two kinds of women, as you think of them. I'd put it this way: there are mature, healthy women who are honest about themselves and their sexual needs and know what they want and when the right man comes along give themselves not only emotionally but in every manner possible; then there are the emotional children, the unrealistic adults who are afraid of life and afraid of living. What do you want? A child or a woman as a wife?

"It's as simple as that, Hank. Because, remember this: a woman who gives herself to a lover, whom she is dating and having romance with, is not a tramp but a woman who is not afraid to be mature—who is sure of herself and not frightened that if she lets a man make love to her, she will lose him. Such a mature woman would be quite happy to discover that the man really didn't care enough—that by letting him have her, he revealed his true lack of love. A woman, when she gets married, wants to be sure of her man, and she doesn't want to capture or trap him by denying a total relationship before marriage.

"To be truthful, I don't know of a married woman who didn't have sexual relations with her husband before marriage! Maybe I just run around with the wrong crowd. But I'll tell you this much, the ones who did give themselves totally before marriage usually ended up with a more healthy union—and not in the divorce courts.

"But don't get me wrong, Hank, I'm not advising such things, I'm not suggesting that this is the only way to a happy marriage. Everybody has to find their own way. All I can say is that the women you seem to fall in love with—and, as you say, don't make love to—are saying no, probably because they aren't sure of you. Why don't you give them a chance, on their terms, because you might discover they are more than you can handle. From what you've told me, you're afraid to make the advances and want the woman to do all the work. Did you ever think that the woman wants to know that her man desires her, that he can't control himself because she's so exciting? If she puts up the stops— fine and dandy. But it's up to her to stop him if she wants to."

Hank considered what I had told him, and then finally said: "You make one hell of a lot of sense. Maybe I'll try that on Mabel, that's the girl I was telling you about. Maybe I'll just call her up tomorrow and see if we can start things again. Maybe you're right.'

Hank left a short time later. It was some months before I heard from him again. He stopped by the apartment one evening about six-thirty, bringing a bottle of expensive scotch whiskey.

"What's the celebration for?" I inquired, starting to open the bottle, "Nothing for me. I'm picking up Mabel."

"Oh?"

"That's the girl I told you about. A woman…a real wonderful woman."

"You're getting along?"

"Wonderfully," he announced with a grin.

I looked at him, silently questioning.

"You were right, Carson. At least you were right insofar as I'm concerned. I called Mabel and we saw each other and we started dating. At first it was much the same as before. Then one night I invited her to my place for dinner. We ate, had champagne, candlelight, and I told her I loved her very much and then pulled her into my arms, kissing her lips eagerly. She melted against me, murmured that she liked me a lot, but that I shouldn't get too serious about her. 'We really hardly knew each other,' she stated, looking into my eyes. But there was a light in hers which seemed to indicate that she wanted to know me a lot better.

"I took your suggestion, rolled with the punches. I pulled her into my arms, caressing her breast while kissing her lips. She strained against me, really eagerly, her tongue went deep into my mouth as I caressed her back and breasts. Then I grabbed the bull by the horns and said: 'I want you like hell and back. Oh, how I want you,' She smiled up at me, kissed my lips tenderly, said: 'I want you, too, Hank, I've wanted you for a long time,' Just like that. And we made love like wild. The funny virgin, it didn't matter that she let me make love virgin, it didn't matter that she let me make love to her—in fact it was the most wonderful thing I'd ever experienced. I...well, found it great, loving her—really, tenderly loving her. It was totally different from the other women I'd had in the past."

He hesitated, looked at his watch, started for the door, and said as a parting shot: "Oh, by the way, we're getting married in a few weeks—want you to be the best man."

CHAPTER TEN

The Extra Martial Affairs: Gale

"I don't know how it really happened, come to think of it," Gale said about her first extramarital experiences. "How does one explain it even to themselves in those non-word thoughts, let alone be able to explain it to another in words?"

I sat opposite her in the neat little white kitchen, the tape recorder between us. Gale's long blonde hair fell flowingly over her shoulders. She was a nicely shaped woman, very attractive even for a woman ten years younger. Gale is a housewife in her middle thirties, full breasted, tallish. The house robe which fell casually around her body gave no indication of what was on underneath. She leaned across the breakfast table, elbow supporting her, holding a cigarette, coffee only inches away from her right hand,

I said, fingering my coffee cup, "Can you explain why it happened?"

"That's even harder," she admitted, with a little nervous shake of her head. "I mean, well, I've been happily married for...well, I met Jim when I was seventeen. We dated for a long time, he went into the service and when he came home on leave, we got married. Our wedding night was the first time I'd seen a man naked. I didn't know what was... well, between his legs, really—only what I'd heard, but seeing is believing, you know."

She looked down at her coffee, embarrassed. "Really, it's going to be hard to talk about it, I think."

I looked at her, wondered how I could break down her hesitation. She wanted to talk about her problem, but was a little shy. We really didn't know each other that well, yet. We had mutual friends and been to several parties with one another. Once, when dancing together, she had been rather sexy, putting her hips tight against mine, later pushing her full thigh between my legs. It was obvious what she was searching for that time. This was morning and at such hours things are a little different."

"Could I suggest something?" I asked, studying her carefully.

"What?"

"Maybe if you had something to drink." She looked up, smiled, said: "Drinking does something to me, Carson...I don't think...."

"What does it do?"

She laughed. "Makes me high!"

"Isn't that what it's supposed to do?" I countered with some humor. "Actually, I thought it would loosen you up a bit."

She gave me a strange look, as if not sure what I meant, then said, after wetting her full lips with a pink tipped tongue: "It might make me *too* loose. That's what happened the first time. I was lonely,

140

frustrated, the kids away at school, Jim off to work, and Joe, next door stepping in for something or other and we talked. I offered him a drink and one thing led to another. Drinks affect me…."

Then suddenly before I could say anything, her eyes studied me very carefully as she said:

"Maybe a drink might help a lot. I think I would like that idea."

She stood and seemed to glide across the room, her hips moving gracefully from side to side far more actively than usually. She disappeared from the room and then after some time returned, a bottle of whiskey in her hand. She got two glasses from the cupboard and then sat down opposite me, poured two amazingly stiff drinks and explained to me, "I like it straight, I hope you don't mind."

I simply shrugged, took the glass she offered and suddenly found my eyes fastened on her robe, where it seemed more open at the top. I could now see for the first time that it appeared there she wasn't wearing any bra or anything under her robe. I wondered if she had done something more than get the bottle of whiskey. The full supple curve of her breasts was openly exposed to my view. Suddenly I began to find myself thinking about this woman in a sexual way, wondering what she was like in bed. The fact that Gale admitted to many extra-marital affairs sent a spark of excitement through me. It was difficult to keep from being highly attracted to her; she was a very mature and desirable woman.

Gale said: "I want you to know that I'm a re-spectable woman. All my life I've loved my children, I was faithful to my husband for years—why I've suddenly changed...I don't know—and that's bothering me. Jim has never slept out on me, I'm sure of that. It isn't jealousy—there isn't any motive other than the fact that, well...I just wanted you to know."

She swallowed hard on her whiskey, stared at me for a considerable time, said: "Carson, I just don't know where to start, and I realize what you want and I just can't talk in that way until...to be honest, until I feel bitchy enough."

She flushed at her last two words, looked down at the drink, then back up into my eyes. "I realize we're alone and that anything I tell you will be...not identified with me—but still...it's difficult to talk to a man who seems a total stranger to me."

"What do you suggest?" I inquired, suddenly guessing what it was and finding the idea strangely stimulating. I'd never been the kind of man to sleep with another man's wife. And to be frank I didn't have any plans on breaking that rule now. No matter what she did, I was here to listen and record her story, nothing more.

She continued to look at me and then finally sighed. "Carson...you're a mature man—you know a lot about life and people. I guess nothing would startle you very much. I guess you've known all kinds of women and men and I guess there's nothing I could do or say that would embarrass or shock you. Isn't that true?"

I nodded, looked down at my drink, took a swallow, and then lighted a cigarette in order to give myself something to do.

"Carson...would you be surprised if I told you...that the other night...at the party, I mean... when we were dancing...I got real charged up—I could tell you were charged up, too."

I glanced at Gale and found myself looking at a woman who had suddenly become topless, rather, her robe was off her shoulders, down to her waist and the large exposed breasts seemed to be calling at me.

She said: "I think I feel bitchy, now. I told you the drinks would get to me. I warned you, Carson. I just don't know how else to put it to you. I would imagine you know what I want—maybe after that, it would be easier to tell you about the other men."

I gaped at her, swallowed hard, and just sat there, not moving, paralyzed to the breakfast nook, afraid to move, afraid to think, afraid to say anything.

She suddenly stood and with one quick action of her hips, she lowered the robe to the floor. She was totally naked.

"Carson...please, I'm aroused and I'm ready and I want you to take me...then I'll be able to talk. I have to tell somebody all about myself—and I have to do it right, but I can't until—it's just a little favor." I was stunned by her approach, but highly effected.

This had happened so fast, yet it was not unexpected, considering the type of woman she had become. She looked at the extramarital relationships as something dirty and like a person who has fallen in shit, believed that she couldn't get any more dirty no matter what she did. She needed to talk to somebody about her sexual adventures, but found it difficult to communicate as boldly as necessary in order to get the results needed. Her offer was natural for Gale, no more guilty by bluntly offering herself in this manner to me than she did about her other affairs, so she had taken the bull by the horns and made a direct play, no little childish games. *I want to have sex with you, so let's get on with it,* was her attitude.

Gale moved over to my side and then took my hand. "Come on, Carson, let's not be childish. Let's get it over with right now."

Like a zombie, I stood, unable to ignore her wanton call. She led me out of the kitchen and through the back porch, into the small half-bath and to a den, in which a large studio couch had been pulled out to make a fairly comfortable surface for two lovers.

She pressed herself against me, circling my neck with her naked arms. "You are getting hard, already," she said, wiggling against me. "Oh, that feels great. Let's get it out." She retreated a little, unzipped me, struggled to get my underpants down and then caressingly held my penis in her now hot, moist hands. She fondled me as if she had discovered the most beautiful treasure in the world and just wanted to love it with wild tenderness.

"I want that inside me, baby," she said, placing it against her genitalia.

We lay down next to each other and then she suddenly said: "Let's do a 69 first. I'll do you while you're doing me. I love to be eaten."

The change in her language was startling. At first she had been shy, afraid to talk about sex, now she found it not only possible, but quite easy to use the most vivid means of communicating her ideas. "I'm clean, lover—I washed myself completely— and I don't care about you one way or the other. I like the smell of a man. Would you do it for me?"

Suddenly she was astride me and I performed cunnilingus on her, while she did fellatio.

The movements became faster and faster as she sobbed and groaned. Then her hands clutched my shoulders, her lips tensed, she rammed hard against me, screamed, "Now, oh, now, flood it in me." But I was already doing exactly that.

Afterward she moved away and lay down on the couch, satisfied. It was some time before she moved, but finally Gale sat up, said: "Well, Carson, let's get on with it."

She left the couch and went into the bath room. We then went into the kitchen. Once again dressed, she sat opposite me, sipping her coffee.

"You know, that made a lot of difference. Now I can say all the dirty words, I can tell you just about anything you want to know."

She smiled and then took another sip of her coffee. "What do you want to know?"

"Start with the first time," I said, a little self conscious about what had happened. She had taken me like a steamroller.

"That was with the guy next door, and I was drunk and lonely and he was a cad. Well, let's put it this way: he's married to a very nice woman and... well, he sleeps out on her—and she knows about it and...well, I guess I'm no better, come to think of it."

"How'd it happen?"

"Joe saw I was drunk, in a house robe and he just started to crowd me. That was after I'd offered him a drink—simply because it wasn't very polite to drink in front of him. He then started to push me—

like standing very close, almost touching, pushing me back against the sink—and I keep trying to keep a polite distance. Suddenly he said, 'You're a most attractive woman.' I thanked him in a very polite, formal way. Then all at once he pulled me into his arms, crushed his lips against mine. I struggled, startled and frightened, not knowing what to do. This kind of thing can happen to a woman, and it usually does happen to most women one time or another in her life.

"I was alone in the house and he knew the kids wouldn't be coming home until late. I'd noticed him many times when he worked in his backyard. Joe was very muscular, well built as hell, exciting to watch and I'd felt guilty at watching him, wondering what he might be like in bed and knowing he slept out on his wife and...well, he killed me with the kiss. Just killed me. I was ready to go. But I fought him off, and we stood there looking at each other, panting, both excited to the point of no return, you can bet your sweet ass on that." She laughed. "I was homey as hell. The funny thing is that I'd never had a satisfactory relation with Jim—I didn't tell you that, did I? Well, I'll tell you all about that later. Right now, let's continue with Joe. Joe was also ready to go. You should have seen the size of him. He looked into my eyes, said: 'Gale...I've wanted to do that for months. You have a delicious looking mouth.' I stood there, staring at him, not able to say anything. He continued with: 'You turn me on, really turn me on.' Finally I found it possible to speak. 'I think you better leave.' He smiled, moved close, pressed his cock against me, and before I knew it he was thrusting at me. 'I know you want that, Gale, just like I want you.' Then he pulled me into his arms, kissed my lips, stuck his tongue deep into my mouth and then started to fondle my breasts. I was so hot that I couldn't stand it. I found myself responding uncontrollably. His body was hard all over and the muscles seemed to twitch with excitement. I thought I was doing this to him, and it was my body which was driving him beyond the line of politeness. He was out of his mind with desire. Desire for me. And he was so strong, like a hard vice all around me. I felt deliciously helpless.

"This idea excited me, plus, of course his throbbing cock. But I said: 'Please, don't…don't...I don't want....' He laughed, driving me insane with his fingers, 'How much would you be willing to bet you don't want it?'

"Well, I didn't even get a chance to really consider it. All I could think of was how good his hand felt and I'd always wondered if there was something wrong with me. I thought that sex was one of those things a woman had to put up with—but that they weren't supposed to *like* it. A lot of women fake it. Orgasm I mean. And men don't know the difference if a woman is any good at it. I thought that was the norm. Suddenly what I was feeling was something totally different from anything I'd ever experienced before."

She paused and said: "You see, when I was married I knew nothing about sex, and Jim is—was then and still is, a little stupid about women. I don't mean that he's dumb—he's very smart, but he doesn't know how to please a woman—he just goes at me. The night of our wedding he climbed on to me, kissed me, pulled up my night gown and proceeded to nuzzle my breasts and fondle me below. Nothing happened to me. The next second he was inside me and, like a jack rabbit, he came two seconds later—leaving me climbing the walls."

She sighed, said: "It's been that way all our married life. I never enjoyed it with him and thought there was nothing more to it. Jim came from a family which didn't talk about sex and he was pretty idealistic and he thought I was enjoying myself— and I've never told him differently. I love him too much to tell him...so we never broke the habit—not even now. I can't talk to him the way I talk to you or some other man I've had sex with. I've tried, so help me, I've tried like hell, but I just can't. I know it would hurt his pride...and I *can't* do that! So, instead, I end up balling it with some other guy for kicks and giving myself to my husband as a wife is supposed to do. Strange, isn't it?"

She was thoughtful for a moment. She lighted a cigarette and blew smoke across the table. "Joe laid me ten places to one. I'd never experienced anything like it before. He just kept his hand on my crotch, so that I just couldn't find the will to stop him and finally I thought, *to hell with* it! I was now so excited I couldn't think of anything but letting him have me, if that's what he wanted. So we went into the den and he undressed me, so skillfully, so thrillingly that I almost had a come from that. When he placed his fingers in my honey pot, I flipped! I had the orgasm of the century.

"When he withdrew I was so overcome with joy and gratitude that I just had to lean down and kiss it. Oh, how I kissed it! I wanted to feed on his cock forever, just so thrillingly out of my mind.

"When he left me that afternoon, I got smashing drunk, sick and shocked at what had happened. I was so dazed by this new discovery that I...well, I was ashamed, and a little mad at Joe and even more mad and disappointed in my husband for never having given me such voluptuous pleasure as that. I decided that the next time I had it with my husband, I'd start leading the way. But the next time I started to let Jim have me, I just froze up. I began to reach for his cock, but I just froze and he was in me and it was over and I was sick at myself. I tried to start a conversation with him, but couldn't. The next day I thought I'd get Joe to come over, but he was out of town and I had to carry on a long, boring conversation with his wife. In the afternoon it was too late to do anything else. I just was one frustrated woman. My Jim called up from the office saying he would be late, very late at work. So I called up a baby sitter, claiming I would go to a movie and went to a bar, picked up a man and we went to a motel. He was surprised at my boldness. I just grabbed him and started fondling, doing all the things I wanted to do with Jim. I then got down on my knees and started really working it over with my lips and had an orgasm when he went off right deep in my... throat. That was really something, feeling him belching and jerking, feeling his cock spasm between my lips, the head...well, I just love giving head and feeling a man's hot, hard, bloody prick going off between my lips, deep in me. Love the taste of come. It's...well...never mind. Just thinking about it makes me...hot all over. I like it in my... well...down there. My...pussy! Just, oh, doing my pussy up hard and hot. I just love it. Anyway, this guy was pretty okay. We had one hell of a session. He was pretty good—not as good as Joe, though, but a lot better than Jim. He managed to satisfy me. I never saw him again, though."

"Is that the extent of your experiences?" I asked.

"No. Every chance I get I pick up a stud. Some times I can't get enough. I have to get me a nice wild...fuck! Love that word. Just love fucking! One time one left twenty dollars and I got the idea of maybe getting more money this way. That's the thing which makes me feel cheap and dirty as hell— but why not take money for what I'm giving out free. It pays for the extra booze that Jim doesn't know about and then I manage to get a few things for myself—Jim thinks I'm getting very thrifty. I ball it with some guy one time a week, at least, during the day or when Jim works late at night."

"You just can't tell your husband about what has happened? You can't suggest that your sex life with him is...unsatisfactory?"

"No—I've tried to tell him—but the words won't come out."

"Did you...well, let's put it this way: You believe your husband loves you?"

"Of course. I'm sure of that. We've had a wonderful marriage. He's very romantic and will never forget a wedding anniversary or birthday or anything—even on holidays he'll bring me gifts. He'll send flowers home at least once a week. He loves me, I'm sure of that. On an emotional side things couldn't be better. But I just love sex! But with a good lover. Somebody who knows how to satisfy me. Jim is like a rabbit. I'm sorry to say."

"Did you ever consider he might want to sexually please you? You said he never had any experience to speak of before marrying you."

"None whatsoever."

"Then, maybe he doesn't realize you are not reacting normally. Maybe if he knew this he'd be more than willing to learn *how* to please you. Did you ever think about that?"

"Yes...but I can't tell him."

"Sometimes it takes an outsider to put people straight."

"Would you tell him?" she suddenly blurted out.

"I don't think that would be a very good idea—he'd punch me in the nose, probably."

Gale laughed bitterly. "Yes, you're right."

"I know several people who would be able to tell him in the right way—it's their job to help people with troubles such as you have. A professional is always ready and willing and able to help couple adjust to one another. They can tell each one the problems involved, they can instruct each in such a manner that nobody gets hurt. They can let your husband realize the truth and the reasons you have never been able to tell him. And in such a manner that he won't feel guilty or ashamed, but actually grateful that somebody could tell him, let him know the truth. Any man who loves his wife wants to give her pleasure, wants to let her know he loves her—that's the difference between a sex party and a marriage.

"In a sex party it is usually selfish—in a love affair—as a good marriage should be at all times—it is an act of giving and sharing in the total intimate way two lovers can enjoy and share one another. Love without sex is bad, and sex without love is bad. But sex with love is what marriage is partly about. You've been missing more than orgasms... your relationship with other men is just orgasms— sexual adventures that would be far more rewarding with the man you love. Is that not right?"

She nodded to that, finished her coffee, lighted another cigarette, and then looked up at me.

I suggested a man I knew who could help her, whom I felt might be the best person to handle her case, and Gale jumped at the chance.

COMMENT

Some months ago I learned that Gale had found a satisfactory relationship with her husband—but not from her, but the man she went to. He said, upon my question about Gale, "Such information is not for the public, only between the people involved, but considering the situation I can tell you this much: Gale and her husband have adjusted beautifully. It turned out that Jim had never been sure she enjoyed sex, and he had done everything possible to makeup for it. He loved her very much and was very happy to discover what had been wrong. Like she told you, she was not a fool, just inexperienced and a romantic. The last session was with Gale and she said there wasn't any reason to keep coming to me any longer, because everything was working out just swell. I'd given both of them several good books on sexology to read and they have been experimenting and gaining a good, balanced sex life. I'm happy with the results."

CHAPTER ELEVEN

Fred

This interview took place some years before the AIDS scare became a harsh reality. It shows how life was on some campuses throughout the country in those wild, free years. People could enjoy a far less guarded sex-life, without modern day concerns about safe-sex. Aids had not raised its ugly head.

Because of the Pill, women were able to enjoy a life-style their mother's had never been able to admit to. It was an experimental time when people were fighting the prudish ethics of earlier generations. Hypocrisy had shaded what really went on behind closed doors.

The sexual drive overpowers reason and logic and legal restrictions. And this case history stands fairly well-centered even today. Students will flaunt their lovely young bodies before their teachers, even offering sexual favors in exchange for better grades or just for kicks. Sometimes it is a power play; sometimes merely a natural attraction for an older lover. But it is a dangerous flirtation many teachers have to squash—or pay a heavy price.

* * * * * * *

Fred looked beady-eyed at me for a moment, lighted his pipe and then after a couple of deep puffs, he shrugged and leaned back in the over-stuffed leather chair centered in his book-lined study.

"I find it difficult to believe it all happened so fast," he told me quite seriously. "One day I'm up for a professorship and then the next day I'm out on my ear. Oh, I'll be able to get some teaching job in a second rate, backwoods college, which will keep me under total control...for a while. But I know it will start all over again."

I studied Fred, an intelligent looking, and serious man in his late thirties, with dark wavy hair that was graying at the temples. Fred is a tall, nicely built man with a handsome face. It was difficult to believe he had allowed himself to get into such trouble.

"Just how did it start?" I inquired.

"I've tried to pin it down—attempted to make sense out of it all. There really wasn't any actual instant, which I can honestly state, was the beginning."

"But surely there was a first—"

"Girl? Yes. There was a first one, and she was a beauty. But it all started long before that. Possibly with my late wife. Maybe even earlier than that. I really don't know. You see," he said, after taking another puff on his pipe, "these young girls are always making innocent flirtations with the teacher, from the eighth grade on...but one gets used to it and learns to simply ignore their provocative bottoms and jutting breasts. It's part of the job. And any teacher caught making the scene with a student is just asking for trouble."

"If you realized this, how did it happen?"

"Over a long period of time. While I was teaching in high school, I was happily married, though to be honest, my sex life with Mary was pretty shoddy...but that's beside the point." He shook his head, stabbed the air with his pipe stem.

"No! That's not quite right. I think maybe that was part of it, I'm not sure. Mary always thought of sex as being...well, something she had to suffer through as a wife. I don't think she really enjoyed sex, though I'm sure she achieved consummation. My thoughts on this is that Mary was ashamed of her sexual side, thought of it as being dirty, and couldn't emotionally accept the idea of liking sexual intercourse. Our sex life was pretty banal, like I said. And at school there was this plethora of tempting pretties doing everything imaginable to catch my eye. There were many times I was quite sure it would be very easy to fix myself up with a girl. Oh, one hears about which girls will and which won't. Plus, you can pretty much tell by the way a girl makes up her face and dresses. The ones with tight skirts, which show off the line of their garter belts...dressing older for their age...with heavy lipstick and eye-make up and wiggling their taunt bottoms...one can tell. Then a teacher will hear about any girl who gets caught or in trouble.

"I heard about this sweet young girl—who didn't dress sexy, actually very sloppy, who was caught in the boy's head, gang-banging. It really ripped the school in two parts. We learned that she had been had by just about every boy on campus—that is, the ones who were looking for a piece. Then one day I got involved in driving this girl home. It was an accident—or was I just tormenting myself? Oh well, I don't know for sure...probably. The thing is that I saw her waiting for the bus one Saturday and pulled up to the curb, said, 'Want a lift?' She jumped at the offer and slipped over pretty close to me. We drove a short distance and she said: 'About that trouble in school...I guess everybody thinks I'm a tramp.' I said something to the effect that her only trouble was not knowing how to handle adult desires. I tried to soothe her. But she merely laughed, said: 'I like it...I just can't help it. I like to you know what...and I really dig you, professor.' I deflected the conversation right there and was quite happy when I managed to get her home.

"But I thought about the obvious fact that I could have made the scene—as they say—with her and nobody would have known better. It bothered me for several days. I guess that's where it began, really.

"When I was boosted up to college teaching, it became even more difficult. My wife was ill and died during the first year at college. That made it even harder. The girls...there were a lot...began to put on the pressure. I learned there were several who had pretty lousy reputations. There was one named Julie, dark haired, tallish, full breasted, who did everything to make herself look trampish. She got in trouble with the school authorities for dressing too revealing and had to tone down her low-necked sweaters. I'd had her in one of my English classes for some time and she wore this low-cut dress that made it possible to almost see down to her navel. And she sat right under me. I'd get a hard on just standing there over her. After school she would dress even wilder. I heard from one of the older teachers that she was a real slut. Then one night I went to one of the beer parlors, feeling restless and...quite honestly wanting a woman. But I didn't have any plans on picking some girl up. I sat in one of the corner tables and drank my beer, listening to the lively music blaring from the juke-box, watching the boys and girls dancing their primitive sexual rites, bodies jerking, breasts bouncing.

"Julie came in with a gang of kids and they seated themselves at a table not far from mine. When Julie spotted me she came over, said:

"'Say, professor, surprise seeing you here.' She sat down giving me a come-on look which would have burned any man. She pushed her knees under the table so that they touched mine.

She was dressed in a tight fitting blouse which was open at the top, giving an excellent view of her breasts. Her lips were full, red, voluptuous, her eyes dark and wild. 'What you doing here, professor?' she asked. I merely said I was having a beer. 'Why don't you join us? The kids would get a kick out of it...and we're going up to my place in an hour or so...you could come along.' I shook my head, thanked her, saying that I'd have to get up early for class. She laughed, hit me with: 'Come on...you might learn something about us students that you don't know. I mean...it's only fair that the student does a little teaching, too. And I can't stand the idea of you being here all alone. Come on.'

"I suggested that the others might not want me with them, and she laughed, stating that it didn't matter...and they expected her to bring me over. 'Sort of a challenge. You don't want me to lose my reputation with them, do you?' She grabbed my hand and her fingers were so soft, warm and sensual that I couldn't resist. I felt like a fool. I mean, I had no idea what she was really trying to do. Make the teach look stupid? A puppy slinking after her hot body? But, I was seduced by her mere hand in mine. We joined the rest of her friends and they seemed to be delighted to have me there. No issue was made of the fact that I was older or that I was a teacher. They accepted me. Julie managed to force me onto the dance floor and we did some of those crazy dances that are vogue now. She jerked and her face glistened; her breasts shook, her hips really did things which shouldn't have been done in public. I attempted to follow and in an awkward, stumbling way I found I got pretty excited watching her dance. The looks she gave me left nothing to my imagination. She was out to seduce me and nothing would stand in her way. Either that or make a bloody fool out of me in the eyes of her friends. By that time I didn't even care; just feasting on her body in such an openly enjoyable way—that was something!

"After about an hour, Julie suggested that everybody come up to her apartment. We vacated the place and went a couple of blocks down the street to where Julie lived. She had a swinging pad, as they say. There were three rooms, with throw rugs, sofas, couches; she had travel posters plastered on the walls. Julie put on the record player, brought out several bottles from the kitchen and then the party was on. I was pretty high by the time one of the boys suggested they really start the party.

"Julie, who was at my side almost all of the time, cried out in delight and suddenly began to take off her blouse, starting to jerk and sway to the music. One of the other girls followed her example right off and the two began a strip show that made professional strippers seem like innocent children. The other girls were beginning to strip down to the music by the time Julie had pulled off her bra. Her breasts were the most lovely, wild things I'd ever seen. They bounced and bobbed, their nipples like little eyes winking and blinking as she jerked to the music. By the time she had pulled off her skirt and slipped out of the garter, the other girls were bare to the waist. There were about ten people there in her place that night and the boys just watched as the five girls went through their strip show.

"I'd heard about such parties, but never in my life expected to be a witness to one; or a part of it. I realized the danger I was in, but didn't give a damn. I was so tight against my pants at just watching Julie, who kept her eyes fastened to mine all the time she was stripping, that I could hardly stand it. Julie made no attempt to hide the fact that she was directing all her plays toward me. As far as she was concerned, I was the only man in the room. I just kept watching her, wondering how far she would undress, not guessing that it would be all the way.

"When she slipped her fingers under the elastic band of the panties and started to peel them downwards, I almost choked in surprise. Then she stepped out of her panties, and totally naked, said: 'Come on, teach, time for you to join me!' She wig-

159

gled her wide hips and started to reach out. In rhythm with the music she slowly, caressing undressed me. When her hands went to my pants, she reached down lower and placed her hand on my testes and penis, massaging it and caressing, all the time looking up at me, with a burning, knowing smile on her lips. She winked, moistened her lips and then unlatched my belt, unzipped the pants, and pushed them downwards, all the time slowly lowering herself to a crouching position. To my profound surprise she proceeded to place my member in her upper orifice—mouth, in other words. I just stood there, paralyzed. I looked around at the others, to find that they were already in different stages of sexual activity, totally ignorant of the other couples around them.

"Slowly, Julie stood, letting her lips and tongue run the full length of my body until they met mine, all the time her breasts following the course of those voluptuous lips. When we kissed, she was flush against me, and somehow she managed to get my penis between her lavish limbs, which squeezed together about the hard shaft. Her tongue was like hot fire as it rapidly went into my mouth, time and time again, all the while moving her thighs in such a way that they were almost jerking me off. I was totally overcome by what was happening and didn't care about anything other than having a real good...hell, I wanted to fuck the wall! Let along her! I couldn't wait to get into her. I was hurting so bloody hard....

"Suddenly Julie lifted slightly and I felt my penis touch the entrance to her vagina, which was as soft and moist as a dewy flower.

"It's hard as hell to get in a girl when both of

you are standing, unless the girl is tall enough—well...a lot of things...but I'll tell you that I'd never experienced anything like this.

"She was holding me in her, deep, all the time kissing me, her tongue flitting in and out of my mouth, faster and faster, her stomach flush against mine. Oh, I'll tell you, it was superb. We just stood there kissing and kissing totally united but doing nothing about it but kissing. Then suddenly I felt her tense all over and her hips jerked wildly against mine, convulsively and I felt myself come like that. It felt as if her insides had simply sucked on me, almost gulping. Well, okay. Illusions, I admit. But, darn if she wasn't just about the best thing that had ever happened to me up to that point! I mean, this was...something totally alien to anything I'd known before. She hugged herself to me, sobbing, clutching, and biting my shoulder with violent passion as we stood there totally smothered in our mutual orgasm. Then she sobbed in my ear: 'You're the greatest, professor. Give me an older man every time.'

"This was some party. The other kids were doing it more conventionally. One couple was lying on the floor, sixty-nining it, I believe is the term. Another was on the sofa, the girl on top, sitting on the man's penis, just rolling from side to side. I could see the expression on her face and it was pure, wild joy, most beautiful! She had her eyes closed, her lips were softly moaning, and she just swayed back and forth, savoring the sensations coursing through her. Suddenly she clutched the boy's thighs, seemed to have a spasm and then continued the peaceful swaying. Across the room was another couple, the girl leaning over, resting her hands on the chair, while the young man mounted her. He evidently came and she laughed, turned around and pulled his limp penis into her mouth. He just stood there enjoying her blow job, which seemed to get almost immediate results.

"All of this time, Julie was swaying, moving, slowly circling her hips, sending erotic sensations through the two of us like charges of electricity. Finally she lifted away, before either of us went off, and then talking hold of my penis, she urged me across the room, leading me like a man on a leash.

"We went into another room, where there was a bed. She sat down on the bed, spread her legs, and then after orally sensitizing my penis for a couple of seconds, we coupled. And when we came we came in tidal waves.

"I lost consciousness and the next thing I knew somebody was playing with my penis. I opened my eyes, thinking it was Julie, but discovered it was one of the other girls, There were two girls in the room with me.

Julie came in just as one girl was preparing to come. She was holding a belt and slapped it across the rear end of the girl working on me. Then as this girl left, Julie slapped the strap across the other girl's back. Julie cried: 'You bitches! Get the hell out of here! He's mine. I claim him for myself!' But the way she spoke, and the way the two girls responded in high pitched giggles, made it obvious that Julie was playing out some kind of rites that all understood and liked. Then she slapped the strap across my chest and sobbing with delight flung herself on top of me, covering my lips with aquatic kisses.

"It was a long night," he admitted with a sigh.

"You stayed with Julie?"

"All night. The others left and I slept with Julie all night—or rather had sex with her and rested in-between. I was absolutely depleted the next morning, so called up and said I was sick. Julie stayed home that day and we continued with the wild sex, only stopping for food and rest and drinks."

"Weren't you afraid of being discovered?"

"I just didn't think about it in any way. And I simply didn't care. I was totally and completely hypnotized with seeming endless hunger for what this girl was offering up on the platter of her quite lush and unrestraint body. I didn't care about anything else in the world! I couldn't get enough…well, put down and dirty: feasting on her!"

"How could you avoid being worried? You're a teacher and there are hard rules against seducing students."

"I couldn't help myself. I was totally captured by Julie's body and wanton sexuality. How I managed to keep up with her is really Julie's fault. She knew more tricks about how to get a rise out of a man—and she was understanding when it was impossible to rise to the stimulation and would find other ways to keep us entertained and excited until I was able to rise up."

"How long did it last? You had to go home, finally."

"Yes, late the next night."

"Did you ever sleep with Julie again?"

"No. I kept away from her, and she seemed to want it that way. We had exhausted each other and there was little interest left."

"But you found other girls interesting?"

"Yes."

"And you apparently had relations with them?"

"Many. That's the trouble. Julie was only first."

"Weren't you afraid that something would happen to...?"

"I was scared silly about being discovered, if that's what you mean. The trouble is that I could not stop once it started."

"How do you mean?"

"I tried. After the Julie affair, I kept out of the way of the young girls for some weeks. I continued to date one of the teachers I'd been dating off and on before. Then one night we went to bed together and it seemed dull, uninteresting. She was too normal, too, too controlled. I craved the wildness and loose freedom of the sexual relations with the young girls. When one young girl made it obvious that she was interested in me, saying that she knew Julie and knew what had happened, I found myself offering to help her with her home work. I couldn't...avoid the temptation.

"She was living off campus and I went to her apartment, feeling like a sneak-thief. She was totally naked when I arrived. There was no playing around with this girl. I'd gained a reputation with a certain element at the college and she was turned on. She claimed that she always went around her apartment, nude. The minute I got into her living room, she came into my arms, said she could hardly wait. We went into the bedroom and had one jolly joust.

"Later, after several drinks and several orgasms, she suggested we call some of her friends over,

164

from across the hall, who were...well...balling it. Once the friends had arrived, stripped down naked, a daisy chain was developed. I presume you know what that means; a group of men and women simultaneously linked together in sexual fusion. I'm sorry to admit...well, I was proud at the time...I lasted longest—probably because of age and more experience...I don't know. The girls would do everything they could to make you go off. That party lasted late into the morning, then after some of the other guys left, because of early classes, their girls started to play games with me...and that was real wild. I'll tell you these girls in this generation are out for kicks and they don't care how they get them! Our society is undergoing a sexual revolution the likes of which is unknown in history. Girls are getting theirs while they can—the guys are getting theirs while they have a chance to live.

"One fellow told me, 'Look, teach, figure it this way: we're all lined up for the army in one way or another—that means we'll be killed and...hell, you only live once and I'm out to get all I can...that *that's* another story!'

"They want to grab as much as they can before it's too late. They act as if there probably won't be a tomorrow—and even if there is, the next day might be the last. They act like people living on a time-bomb. They are more educated about sex and are able to enjoy sexual freedom because of the pills and medical control over social sickness. They flip, jerk, and ball it, openly, freely, happily, grabbing life head on and living *now,* with all their guts.

"One can say people in our generation, and those in the Second World War, and much later than that, were swallowed up by fear, by terror of death—but it was different then. People didn't talk so openly about sex. They didn't read much about it. And what they read was either watered down or some underground 'dirty' book. Now you can get just about everything you want on sex in the book stores, openly. And in a way I believe it's healthier. If you talk about it, have it openly exposed, in time everything will level off to a point where everybody will be sexually healthy—unafraid of exposing themselves emotionally and physically with some-body they love. These kids are, in a way, showing the road to happiness. In a bold, honest, in times crude manner, but they are giving their elders a les-son about life—that you only live once and you might as well make the most of it feeding all your hungers, without guilt, without false pride.

"And, because of that I'm quite sure that I'll fall right back into *living!* I know what it will mean—I know that it will put me out of work—that I'll get fired again—but I hope that in a few years the moral attitude of American society will allow men like myself to indulge openly with adult women—no matter how young, as long as they are legal age, of course—and nobody will give a damned. To be truthful, the older women are dull. Boring! To be frank, too conservative and restricted. What's the word? Hung-up! The younger set knows where they are going and they know what they want. I don't be-lieve they will be frustrated or sexually crippled like their parents were, because they aren't afraid of the pleasures that are theirs for the taking."

"You honestly believe this?" I inquired ser-iously, realizing that in a way he was stating a great partial truth. All the people I'd met, whom I had talked with, felt guilty about their sexual affairs— afraid of sex—ignorant about the causes of their unhappiness, and this was in part caused by a lack of understanding about life, a fear of being alive and in the living experience.

Fred re-lighted his pipe, nodded, and said: "What I did was to live a bit, with young girls who wanted sexual thrills and didn't give a damned how they got them. They're young, but experienced, youthful but adult enough to indulge in total sexual freedom. They don't go out and rape each other on the streets, they merely ball it up in the privacy of their own homes. They are single and have every right to live the kind of lives they wish, just so they aren't hurting anybody but themselves. And they aren't hurting themselves, really, because they can go into a relationship with a guy, without getting themselves involved emotionally...they can look at sex as one hunger—love as another hunger—and they don't get confused. When they meet somebody of the opposite sex they can fall in love with they will probably end up happily married forever. What else do we want?"

I asked Fred how he happened to get caught and he merely smiled, shrugged. "It was easy. In time my reputation had to get noticed by the administration—it did and I was fired."

"Don't you think it's cost you a lot? Don't you think it would be better to have found a normal relationship with a woman your own age?"

"Find me one who has the same sexual attitude as one of these young women of the current generation—the swingers, the hippies, whatever you want

167

to call them—and I'd still probably pick a younger girl…at least for a while. I'm not interested in getting married. I can arrange to have my affairs with any of a dozen young girls—who will even willingly come and live with me for a while. I'm not looking for marriage right now—and it will be a long time before I do."

COMMENT

Fred was getting to that age which is called the dangerous age for men—but he was experiencing it in a manner that most men don't get the chance. The cost, to him, seemed little. To me it seemed a harsh one to pay.

There was no professional help for Fred, simply because he had found an answer that satisfied himself, and he knew the dangers involved and he had accepted an answer which was difficult to defeat, for it pointed to the future, and only the future can reveal the final judgment.

I don't know the answer. Some might say that the United States—and the world—is headed in the same direction as Rome was when it started the mass orgies of death in their arenas. But they didn't have the bomb, they didn't have the cultural history that our new, alive, aware generation was developed upon. A lot has happened in 2,000 years—a lot more will happen in the next twenty. Let's hope that the future will find the perfect balance between love and harmony, romance and realism, peace and prosperity throughout the world—a world of total love, not total fear.

Note added by Carson Davis for this Wildside edition:

The AIDS threat and the change of moral ethics and the strong religious movement in the United States has tempered some of the ideas expressed by Fred and many others like him from his generation. But even with times changing and the necessity of Safe Sex becoming a demand for all concerned in order to have a healthy, and safe relationship with somebody they love, people find a way to express intimacy. Some answers involve no sex. Others enjoy a healthy sex life, but in a safe manner! Condoms are required. The single life has altered time and again. But no matter what the restrictions involved, people find a way to discover one another.

ABOUT THE AUTHOR

Carson Davis is just another pen name for a rather prolific writer who had many other pen names and scores of books published during his writing career.

The author reports that when he started writing his agent told him that the really hungry market for beginning writers was the so-called "adult novels" aimed at male sexual fantasies. This market, over the years, changed dramatically. When his publishers started releasing case-history books he created the Carson Davis name, which appeared on some twenty pocketbooks.

Now Wildside Press is offering a few of Mr. Davis' books to its readership. The realistic grounding of his work is starkly evident. And his continual message reflects a non-judgmental attitude about people's moral ethics.

He writes:

I have lived in Southern California most of my life, and perhaps that has molded my own personal convictions concerning morality. I've experienced marriage in a wonderful way. And like "Carson Davis" I've been convinced that real love and commitment comes when people are willing to share their lives together in an honest and loving manner. How that shapes itself is a matter of each person's beliefs and standards.

These books, under the Carson Davis byline, have always been an especially rewarding experiment, for they gave me a chance to express a lot of basic thoughts and ideas which can't be articulated in straight novels in exactly the same way. In the case history format I was able to examine ideas and concepts that reached across many cultural and religious borders. The only restriction was the theme of each book. Beyond that I could do pretty much what seemed most reasonable.

I didn't depend only on my own knowledge concerning human sexology, but drew upon the excellent advice of a minister and therapist willing to share solid information dealing with the thematic material all of these books covered. Because of this I have felt they offered very important truths about life, sex, relationships and some essential insights into a wide array of thinking concerning the human condition.

I have never talked to a person who was a real pervert or deviant, but rather to many people with different points of view who had something to reveal in their apparent "confessions" about life, sex and what they believed was the ideal solution to just surviving.

It is enough to say these books were popular and have found circulation throughout the world. They stand up today as well as they did when originally published.

www.ingramcontent.com/pod-product-compliance
Lightning Source LLC
Chambersburg PA
CBHW051919240626
47153CB00004B/1282